FUR-MILIAR FELINES

A Wonder Cats Mystery Book 7

HARPER LIN

CONTENTS

Black Aura

"Are you sure you think Jake will like these?" my cousin Bea asked me for the hundredth time as we stood in line at Paige's Neighborhood Store.

Bea held up a pair of red-and-green Christmas socks that had a matching tie and kerchief. Paige's was an old-fashioned country store in the bustling upscale part of town. They carried everything from jewelry to electric fireplaces.

"That isn't all you're getting him, right?" I asked. If that were all I got from my spouse, I'd be a little miffed.

"No. I already got him some of his favorite coffee beans and one of those army-style flashlights like the department gives them. He wanted one of his own. I picked up a new workout suit for him to wear to the gym. There was a sale on boxers and socks, so I stocked up on those for him. And then I also picked up…"

I nodded and adjusted my dusty-pink Santa hat as Bea rambled on all the things she had picked up for her husband. Usually we spent Christmas day with my aunt, Bea's mom, who would cook a fantastic meal that actually included some kind of real meat like lamb or turkey. Had we left it up to Bea, we'd be eating tofu with bean-paste stuffing and a heaping salad of kale. The thought made me wrinkle my nose and swallow hard. Have you ever choked down kale? Ugh.

"But the big gift …well, you'll think it's silly."

"Bea, I'm wearing a Santa hat, and underneath my coat is my favorite ugly Christmas sweater. I'd have a lot of nerve if I thought *anything* was silly."

"Okay, but promise me you won't say anything to Jake about it. He's so sensitive. I don't want him to quit before he ever gets started."

"What? What is it?"

"Well, have you seen those commercials on television for those software programs that you can talk into and they record your words and put them on paper?"

"Yeah." I nodded.

"Well, I bought that for Jake. He wants to write a book." Bea batted her lashes, waiting for my response.

"Really? That's awesome," I said. "I blame you for that. You have a way of making people try creative things they normally wouldn't. Does he want to write crime stories?"

"No. Romance."

"No way!" I cried out, attracting the attention of just about everyone at the store. "That is so great. I want the first copy of every book off the press. I'll be his number-one fan, but not in the creepy way like that woman in that Stephen King story."

Bea laughed.

"I'm so happy you think it's a good idea," Bea gushed. "He's so worried that people will judge him if he's no good."

"Well, he'll never know if he doesn't try. Have you seen some of the stuff out there? Seriously, I doubt Jake could do any worse."

Bea beamed. Then she asked a question I wasn't prepared to answer.

"So? What are you getting for Tom?"

Tom Warner was a police officer. He had beautiful blue eyes and cowboy boots and a red pickup truck, and he knew I was a witch.

Some people hesitate to tell other people they like intimate details about themselves for fear of rejection. Perhaps they worked at a strip club at some time or did drugs at some point. I was a witch. It wasn't something I broadcast. I had learned the hard way that even people you think will accept you unconditionally will back away when they find out you're a witch. It spooks them. But when I told Tom, he didn't get spooked. In fact, he had his own supernatural experiences, so I guess you could say we had that weirdness in common.

"I haven't decided what to get him." I winced, knowing what Bea's response was going to be.

"You haven't? Christmas is only twelve days away."

"I know. But I haven't seen anything that I thought he'd like," I whined. "I am hoping that if I hold out long enough, it'll just come to me. I'll know it when I see it."

"Okay." Bea nodded. "What does he like? Does he prefer a certain kind of music or books or something?"

"Yeah, well, he likes all kinds of music and reads crime and thrillers. You know, guy stuff." I took a deep breath as we inched our way closer to the register. "I'm sure I'll see something that he'll like if I'm just patient."

"Well, he really picked out a beautiful broach for you." Bea tapped the beautiful vintage pin on my peacoat that Tom had surprised me with a couple weeks ago. I blushed as my cousin smiled at my discomfort.

I looked all around the store until my eyes fell on something that was a complete distraction from the current conversation.

There was a marquee covered with flyers of local events for the holiday season. Homemade baked bread and holiday fruitcakes were being sold by Busy Bees over on Tyler Street. Saint Michael the Archangel Church was collecting canned goods and nonperishables from now through the New Year. The Wonder Falls Park District was hosting the Tenth Annual Pet Reindeer Contest.

"Bea, look at this." I pointed to the flyer. "This is Treacle's year."

"Oh, good luck with that." Bea giggled. "Do you think he'll go for it? More importantly, does he think he can beat Peanut Butter as a reindeer?"

"Oh, so that's how it's going to go down." I knew Bea wouldn't be able to resist getting into the act. Her cat, Peanut Butter, was an adorable bundle of orange fur. He was still a kitten compared to Treacle, who was in his healthiest midlife. But he would never look as cool as a reindeer as Treacle would. My cat's black fur and green eyes would look fantastic in a red Santa hat with reindeer horns sticking out of it.

"I don't know if we should tell my mom." Bea squinted.

Marshmallow, a gorgeous gray, pug-nosed Persian, was my aunt's cat. I'd never repeat this to Treacle, but Marshmallow's roly-poly body and beautiful fur made her look like royalty.

"Not if either of us wants to win." I scoffed. "What do you win?"

I continued reading the flyer and in the back of my mind was trying to figure out how I would convince my cat to do this. My witchy gift was that I could communicate with my familiar. Actually, I can communicate with all animals, but cats come through as clear as I was talking with Bea right here next to me. Dogs communicate well if you enjoy talking to toddlers, which I really do sometimes. Wild animals are a little harder to understand but not if you practice a little patience. Needless to say, cats go best with us witches.

"A-ha." I pointed to the flyer. "You win the prestigious title of Pet Reindeer of the Year, a blue ribbon, and a certificate signed by the mayor."

"I mean this with nothing but love and respect," Bea said, "but you are going down."

"You go ahead and think that, Lady Jane." Lady Jane was a term Aunt Astrid would use on both Bea and me when we were in a spot of trouble. I hadn't heard it in years, but it just flew out of my mouth. It made us chuckle.

"You're going to make such a good mother one of these days," Bea said as she riffled through a bin that held various swatches of Christmas fabric scraps.

I blushed.

Just then I noticed two women who looked familiar come up behind Bea. There was a short, heavy woman with a good bit of makeup on, talking intently to a tall, thin woman who preferred the natural look. They both looked very worried.

"I just don't know what to do," the shorter woman stated. "What do you say to a woman whose son is missing?"

"She's got to be frantic. Has she gone to work?" the other woman asked.

"Yeah. The bills don't stop coming. Could you imagine that? Going to work when your son has either run away from home or been taken, Heaven

7

forbid, and being told to return phone calls and file paperwork. I'd totally go postal if I were in that situation."

I looked at Bea and with my eyes indicated for her to listen a little closer. I was always surprised by some of the things you learned while standing in the check-out line.

"My gosh. She's called the police?"

"Yes. They told her that he's probably run away and will be back when he either gets hungry or cold enough," the short woman replied. "You know, he is almost eighteen. The cops won't take mother's intu- ition into consideration. Sad to say."

"What about her ex-husband?"

"Bruce Lyle Sr.?" The shorter woman stated the name that immediately made me look at Bea.

Bea had the luxury of having her back to the women, and her eyes popped as her mouth fell open. Sad to say, we both knew Bruce Lyle.

"Bruce Lyle Sr. is blaming Melissa, saying she is just trying to ruin his Christmas with his new girl- friend." The shorter woman put her hand on her hip. "He hasn't offered to go out looking or put up flyers. Melissa has been doing that every free minute she's had. But no, Bruce can't really be bothered. He can't be bothered searching for his son who has disappeared. Can you believe that?"

"How long has he been missing?" the taller woman asked.

"So far, it's been about a week. He hasn't been at school. Didn't show up at his job. You know, he works at that little coffee place inside the grocery store."

"What do you think happened?" the thinner woman asked as she applied clear Chapstick to her lips.

"I don't know any kid who has a relatively normal life that would take off and run away just a few days before Christmas. Presents? Special dinner? School vacation starts tomorrow, I think. It doesn't make sense."

We finally inched our way up to the register so Bea could pay for Jake's Christmas socks. Before we walked out of the store, we heard one last eerie detail.

"The really weird thing is that Melissa said that none of Bruce Jr.'s clothes were missing. Not only did he not pack anything if he ran away like the police think, but Melissa said none of his shoes are missing, all of his pants are there, and his winter coat is still hanging in the closet."

"Maybe he borrowed a pair of boots or something from a friend," the thin woman said. "Otherwise, you're saying he left the house naked."

"Left or was taken."

The two ladies continued their discussion, and we could no longer eavesdrop without looking like a couple of gossip hens. I linked my arm through Bea's as she finally had her purchase, and we headed out of Paige's. Neither one of us knew what to say.

"Melissa has been in the café a couple of times, but she never said anything," Bea said. "You know, I thought something was wrong with her when she came in. There was a hint of black around her aura, but that is so common around the holidays I just thought she was going through a little bout of holiday blues. My goodness. I could have helped her."

Bea's gift as an empath allowed her to not only sense people's suffering, but also take it on as part of herself. She'll absorb the pain so the other person can maybe get a couple nights' sleep or have a clear mind to figure out what to do. In more extreme cases she can untangle a malicious spirit or a paranormal parasite that might be using the person as a host and send it back to whatever dimension it crawled out of. She's very good at their removal. I should know because she helped me. She should get T-shirts made that read Bea's Supernatural Pest Control.

"What do you say?" I shrugged. "Hey, Merry Christmas and all that jazz, and by the way, my son's gone missing. If you see my Bruce Jr. around, can you tell him to get right home and maybe mention he should put some clothes on?"

"That's weird, right?" Bea shook her head as she climbed into my car, and we headed to the Brew-Ha-Ha Café for the lunch shift. We didn't mention the conversation to Aunt Astrid. We had forgotten about it since there was a fight going on in the café as we arrived.

Fight

✿❀✿

"**E**veryone is considered innocent until proven guilty!" It was Mr. Wayne, a teacher from Bibich High, yelling at a blond man who was being held back by who I could only assume was his wife. "I'll have my day in court. You'll see. Your kid and those others got me fired for nothing!"

Half the patrons had receded to the far wall to stay out of the way but were all too happy to be watching. The remaining people were attempting to keep the two men apart. Aunt Astrid was on the phone, telling the police to hurry.

"You've got a lot of nerve showing your face around here!" The other man lunged at Mr. Wayne. "You put your hands on my son. You pervert! You belong in a cage!"

"There is no proof I've done anything wrong," Mr. Wayne said defiantly. "I'm a taxpayer. I have a right to go wherever I want."

"I'll see that you rot in jail!" The man's face was the angriest red I had ever seen. His eyes watered with tears of fury, and his wife was losing her battle to hold him back.

Thankfully, my dearest friend, Min Park, was in the café this late morning. He and another fellow kept Mr. Wayne at arm's length from his attacker. It was interesting to see Min help, since in high school, he was the one mercilessly bullied. Now, Min has grown to be strong and extremely successful.

With all the people crammed into the Brew-Ha-Ha, Bea and I couldn't get to Aunt Astrid. Bea tried to inch her way to the more aggressive man to put her hands on him. I knew she thought that if she could take away some of his pain, she might be able to calm him down enough until the police arrived.

I, on the other hand, kept looking toward the window for the red and blue lights and listening for the sirens but couldn't see or hear anything over the shenanigans going on.

With one final attempt, the angry man knocked over a couple of our chairs, pushed aside my aunt's favorite table, and almost punched Mr. Wayne across the jaw. Had the man not been off balance, he would have taken out a couple of teeth or broken Mr. Wayne's nose for sure. But it was more of a humiliating brush along the chin than an actual pummeling. However, I knew what would come next. I could tell by the look in Mr. Wayne's eyes. In fact, I think I heard everyone let out a collective groan of disbelief when they heard Mr. Wayne cry out.

"That's it!" Mr. Wayne cried. "I'm going to sue you for assault. You just made a big mistake, pal, and I've got witnesses!"

"Get them out of here!" Aunt Astrid yelled as she held the phone to her ear. "Get both of them out of here!"

Finally, the police arrived in two black-and-white squad cars with sirens blaring and lights rolling. I held the door open for the officers. Bea was finally able to get to her mother and stand protectively in front of her. Some of the gawkers quickly got out of the way, and Mr. Wayne, suddenly unsteady on his feet, holding his jaw and acting as if he were going to faint, let two of the police officers lead him out of the café first. The other two officers went inside to talk to the other man.

I stood with Aunt Astrid and Bea. We all looked

at each other, stunned. I caught Min's eye, and he just shrugged.

"Now, Mr. Mavery, we know you're upset," the first policeman said while he kept his hand on his Taser. "But you need to let the law handle things the right way."

"Why is that monster out?" the angry man demanded.

"Mr. Mavery, did you assault Mr. Wayne?" the officer asked as his partner carefully cleared out the café.

"Yes. I hit him. If I could have gotten closer, I would have strangled the life right out of him. You know what he did to my boy and those others at the school. You know what he did!" Mr. Mavery's voice was low and hateful.

"I'm sorry, Mr. Mavery. Turn around and put your hands behind your back."

Mrs. Mavery started to cry and assured her husband she'd call their lawyer as soon as she got home. She shook her head in disgust.

"You men should be ashamed of yourselves," she spat at the officers after she reassured her husband everything would be all right.

I stretched my neck to see what the police were doing outside with Mr. Wayne and was shocked to see the paramedics pull up. Of course, after getting popped in the face, he had to be put on a stretcher and examined if he was serious about filing a lawsuit.

One police officer led Mr. Mavery out of the café. The other approached Min and some of the people who were still in the far corner of the dining area to get their statements. After, he approached Bea.

"You're the owner?" He took out his pad of paper and a small pencil and looked at Bea. Her bright-red hair and blue eyes were captivating, and it was something to see how some guys would ask the silliest questions just for a chance to chitchat with her.

"No." She shook her head and jerked her thumb behind her. "My mother is." And she stepped aside, letting Aunt Astrid take center stage.

Aunt Astrid told him everything.

Mr. Mavery and his wife had come into the café looking as if they hadn't had a good night's sleep. Their eyes were downcast, and Mrs. Mavery yawned widely as they took a seat next to the window.

"Yes, right over there," Aunt Astrid said to the officer, pointing to the area of the room where several of the tables and chairs had been shoved aside. "Something outside caught Mr. Mavery's attention."

He had been looking out the window as his wife was speaking to him. When she reached for his hands, he took hers and squeezed them tightly.

"I thought he was going to cry, and that led me to think that maybe there had been an unexpected death in the family. But when I saw him jump up, I knew something was wrong."

Just then, Aunt Astrid said, the bells went off over the door and a man had walked in. He looked familiar. She recognized his face from the recent newspaper articles.

Bibich High School was the biggest high school at Wonder Falls, sitting at the edge of town. The girls' volleyball team was regional champ three years ago.

But now Bibich High School was in the newspaper for another reason. Several children, both boys and girls, had come forward, accusing Mr. Gale Wayne of a varying range of offenses, from indecent exposure, to lewd and lascivious behavior in front of a minor, to sexual assault. Their ages ranged from thirteen to seventeen years old. Mr. Wayne had been arrested, but he was released when he made bail. The preliminary hearing was set to take place in the next few weeks.

I hadn't paid much attention to the story. I know it might sound selfish, but I was busy trying to figure out what to get my boyfriend for Christmas. I didn't go to Bibich High School, I didn't know anyone who did, and I didn't have any teenagers in my life who attended that school that I could be worrying over. It was a scandal that didn't apply to me. But now it had literally barged in on my family and me.

"Mr. Wayne walked in. Everyone knew who he was from the paper," Aunt Astrid said. "Mr. Mavery made it pretty obvious that he was the father of one of the boys who had accused Mr. Wayne of... you know."

"Did Mr. Mavery approach Mr. Wayne?" the officer asked.

"No, sir," Aunt Astrid had replied. "It was Mr. Wayne who approached Mr. and Mrs. Mavery. I don't know what he said to them. I couldn't hear. But whatever it was left Mrs. Mavery with her mouth hanging open and Mr. Mavery grabbing hold of Mr. Wayne's collar."

"That isn't what Mr. Wayne reported." The officer looked at my aunt skeptically.

"I saw the whole thing, Officer." Min stepped up. "I was right here at the counter."

The officer nodded and finished taking Aunt Astrid's statement before moving on to Min. Bea and I admitted we had come in after the ruckus had already started and were mostly interested in keeping Aunt Astrid safe.

When the police left, the patrons settled down, although the conversations buzzed louder than usual.

"Jeez, Aunt Astrid. Bea and I go out to do a little Christmas shopping together, and this is what happens," I teased. "This is why we can't have nice things."

"My gosh, Mom," Bea said as she helped me move all of the chairs and tables back to their proper places. "Maybe I've been living in a cave, but I don't know anything about that situation at the high school. Jake hasn't said anything to me. How did you hear about it?"

"It's a recent development," my aunt replied with a tired voice. "I don't know whether it's true or not. I can't tell yet." Her eyes roamed our faces then looked out the window. "But something strange is happening."

Min came by after he finished chatting with the fellow who had helped him hold Mr. Mavery back.

"Well, I hate to witness a brawl and then run. I just stopped by to wish you all a wonderful Christmas. I'm leaving with my parents to go visit some relatives in Hawaii while I do a little business."

"Hawaii for Christmas?" Bea smiled. "Now that sounds wonderful. Safe travels, and a very Merry to your folks from us."

"Well, now, who am I going to drink eggnog and count ugly Christmas sweaters with?" I said. "Hawaii. There's no snow there, huh?"

"Have you ever been?"

"No. And yes, I am terribly jealous. I'm just trying to find the negative side of Christmas in Hawaii to make myself feel better." I laughed and gave my friend a big hug. "When you get back, you might be able to make yourself a couple of extra dollars playing bouncer for Aunt Astrid if the Brew-Ha-Ha continues to live up to its name."

Bea and Astrid said their good-byes to Min.

It would be two days before Bea and I remembered to tell Aunt Astrid what we'd heard about Bruce Lyle. It came rushing back to us when his mother, Melissa, came into the café late one evening.

Missing

✿

Melissa Radke, previously known as Mrs. Bruce Lyle Sr., had gone back to her maiden name as soon as she found out about her husband's indiscretions. When she walked into the Brew-Ha-Ha, my heart broke just looking at her.

Her eyes were weighed down with dark circles, and the rims were red as if she'd been crying. She wore no makeup, and her hair was pulled back in a careless ponytail that offered no complement to her round face.

"Hey, Melissa," I greeted her quietly when she came into the café for her usual black coffee on the way home from her job as a nurse at St. Joe's hospital.

At the café, we had decided to try something a

little different this year and stay open until midnight for the two weeks leading up to Christmas Eve in order to accommodate some of the later-evening shoppers.

Normally we'd see her at three o'clock as she worked the afternoon shift and would be home in time for her son, Bruce Jr., but that had changed. Now she was working the graveyard shift. It was a poor choice of words, but that was what it was.

"Hi, Cath," she said quietly. "Just a black coffee."

"Coming right up." I smiled and bumped Bea to get her to turn around for a second. She might be able to help. She caught on and greeted her.

"Hi, Bea. Say, would you girls do me a favor?"

I nodded, and Bea said, "Of course."

"Would you put this up in your window?" She reached into her purse and pulled out a flyer from a huge stack. It was a picture of Bruce Jr. with the word MISSING across the top.

"Oh dear." I didn't know what else to say. I certainly couldn't say, "Oh yeah, heard some ladies gossiping that your kid went missing. So it's true. Truthfully, I forgot about it up until just now. But yeah, we'll put this in the window." Instead I just followed Bea's lead.

"Dear God," Bea said sadly. "I'm so sorry, Melissa. When was the last time...?"

"I haven't seen him in nine days. He hasn't called. None of his friends have seen him. Or should I say his friend." She swallowed hard. "Bruce is alone a lot. He says he prefers it that way, but I'm not so sure."

Just then, Aunt Astrid came from the kitchen and immediately narrowed her eyes at Melissa, who didn't notice.

"With everything that's been going on at the high school... Bruce was one of those children that said Mr. Wayne..." She couldn't choke out the words. Bea handed Melissa her coffee and quickly took hold of her hand. But Melissa gently pulled away. "I'm sorry," she mumbled. "I know you mean well, but I just can't stand being touched right now. I only want to hug my boy." Her eyes welled up.

"I understand," Bea muttered kindly. "Is there anything we can do?"

"Bruce hated school," Melissa continued absently. "He was having a spot of trouble with another boy. Actually, it's boys. Those kinds of children always travel in packs." She grimaced. "Bruce just wanted to get through high school. His uncle, my brother, had a job waiting for him at a factory in Chicago. I thought it would be great for him to leave the state and go stay with them for a while and get some real life experience on his own. He acted like he couldn't wait. But these kids at school..."

Unfortunately, this story was hitting a nerve with me. Melissa was right. These kinds of children always travelled in packs. They picked on anyone they considered weaker. That was how Darla Castellano did it. She and her best friend, Ruby Connors, the same Ruby Connors whose brother tortured my friend Min, used to hassle me something fierce. There were many times I contemplated running away.

"Bruce's father didn't make things easy for us." I could tell Melissa was holding back from saying what she really thought about her ex-husband. "Things spread all over town, and somehow what my husband did became my son's fault and shame. I tried to tell him that high school was just a blip in his life. That it would be over after one more year and then he'd never have to see any of those people again. But then he said that he had problems with Mr. Wayne, and that hit the headlines. "

She looked up at us from her coffee.

"I'm sorry." She tried to smile. "I don't mean to prattle on."

"Please, Melissa." Aunt Astrid came up to the counter. "You don't have to say you're sorry for being a mother. Leave as many of those flyers as you can with us. We'll get them out. Let Bea make you a tea to take with you. A good night's rest can lead to an idea or solution in the morning. Please."

Before Melissa could put up a fuss, Bea was fixing one of her special elixirs with a few drops of honey, a sprinkling of lavender petals, and a little hocus-pocus. She presented a tall takeout cup to Melissa.

"Thank you." Melissa sniffed, keeping most of her tears back as she handed me a stack of flyers. "What do I owe you?"

"Oh, it's on the house." I waved my hand as if shooing a fly. "Don't worry about it. We'll just take it from Bea's paycheck." I winked.

"Melissa." Bea put her hand gently on Melissa's arm and was nearly knocked off balance by the over-whelming feeling of sadness and desperation. The weight was so heavy I was sure she'd collapse right there, but she held tight. "We mean it when we say if there is anything we can do to help, let us know. Even if you want to just come and prattle on."

I saw the sweat forming on Bea's temple. What-ever she was absorbing was worse than she thought it would be. But still, she held on to Melissa's arm. It looked like nothing more than a simple exchange between friends. But I saw Melissa stand a little straighter as just a small bit of relief came to her spirit.

"Thanks, ladies. I may just do that." She patted Bea's hand before pulling away. Taking her coffee and special tea, she left the café.

"I've got you," Aunt Astrid said as she put her arms around Bea and helped her to the chair at the end of the counter.

"That poor woman." Bea held back tears. "I've never seen that kind of pain before. It's like a flowerbed overrun with thorny, sickly weeds that keep cropping up and choking the new sprouts. Her hope is giving way to despair, and I'm just afraid what will happen if Bruce isn't found."

We sat there for a few minutes, not saying anything but thinking the same thing. Finally, in the most tactful and gentle way I could, I asked the worst question.

"If Bruce Jr. was one of the kids accusing Mr. Wayne of something and Mr. Wayne is out on bail, do you think he could have offed the boy?"

"Offed?" Bea looked at me. "Are you in the Mafia all of a sudden?"

"If I were, I would have said *whacked*. Get with it, Bea."

"It's a possibility." Aunt Astrid's serious tone made my cousin and me stop our bantering. "I can't imagine a teenager willingly running away from home just two weeks before Christmas. Not with the prospect of presents and special dinner and all the stuff that goes with the holiday."

"That's a good point." Bea took a deep breath and smoothed her hair back from her face. She nodded to her mother that she was okay to stand up. "Cath, would you lock the door? I think we've had enough customers for tonight."

"I agree," Aunt Astrid said as she walked to the café windows. "It looks like we might be in for a few flurries tonight." I watched her as she looked outside, and thought she was looking for something or someone. Then I felt a cold chill rush over me.

"Did you guys feel that?" I murmured as I snapped the lock on the door, turned the Yes, We're Open sign to Sorry, We're Closed, and flipped off the front lights. The café was eerily lit by the lights at the back of the café and made it look like an unfriendly, foreign place. Normally, closing up shop never made me nervous. But I felt an urge to hurry up and get going.

"You feel it, too?" Bea asked as she took the receipts from the register along with the deposit that would be dropped off at the bank tomorrow morning. "Kind of feels like we're being watched, doesn't it?"

"Yes," Aunt Astrid said as she closed the blinds. Before I could ask her what she saw or what she was thinking, my aunt turned and smiled at me. "Cath, let Bea take you home tonight. Don't walk by yourself."

"It's okay, Aunt Astrid. You know I like to feel the cold and smell the fireplaces that cut through the air. I don't mind..."

"No. Not tonight," she kindly ordered. I looked at Bea, who shrugged.

"All right, Aunt Astrid. Bea, you mind?"

"Of course not. Why don't you come by for some hot chocolate?"

"It's real hot chocolate, right? It's not some weird, chocolate-ish herb or nut that is healthier but tastes like feet?"

"I've never given you anything that tastes like feet," Bea snapped. "Of course, I never tasted feet, which apparently you have."

We laughed like schoolgirls. We did that often but this time stopped short when Aunt Astrid didn't chuckle along with us. She was nervous about something, but my cousin and I knew better than to pressure her into talking. Aunt Astrid would tell us what was on her mind when she was good and ready, and not a moment sooner.

"Just make sure you and Jake walk her home. Don't go by yourself."

"Why?" Bea asked.

"No reason except to play it safe." Aunt Astrid smiled. She was hiding something. We both knew it but said nothing.

It was really no bother at all to go to Bea's place. We lived just across the street from each other. Aunt Astrid lived on the same block a couple houses over. A perfect equilateral triangle if you had a bird's-eye view.

"Do you want us to stay and walk you home?" I asked. "If you think we should be playing it safe for some reason you aren't telling us? I'm not trying to be a smarty-pants. I'm just saying that..."

"I'll be fine. In fact, I've got a few things to do in the bunker. I probably won't be leaving for another hour or two."

The bunker was a small room off the kitchen that from the outside looked like a supply or utility closet. But when you opened the door and descended the cement steps, you were in a tiny nook filled with some of our favorite spell books and witchy histories.

I was about to protest my aunt staying alone, but judging by the look on her face, I decided I'd better trust her. She didn't look as if she wanted company.

Truthfully, Aunt Astrid was a super-witch compared to Bea and me. She was the last person we really needed to be worried about since she had the gift of seeing what was coming before it arrived. Not to mention the years of experience in spell casting and good old-fashioned charming when necessary. Still, she was my aunt. I loved her and worried anyway.

White Precipitation

❧❀❧

"So why do you think your mom asked us to stick together like this?" I asked Bea as we sat in her kitchen.

Bea had a lovely kitchen that had an island. I sat at one of the barstools and watched her make our hot chocolates.

"I'm not sure," Bea replied. "But I wasn't going to argue with her. Sometimes it's better just to nod and agree. I'm assuming you want mini marshmallows in your hot chocolate."

I nodded. In addition to being an empath, Bea also had a knack for cooking. The only problem with her cooking was that it was usually some odd vegetarian weirdness that included kale and sunflower seeds and a host of things I usually don't think of when deciding what to have for dinner.

My mind is usually on a big, juicy cheeseburger with everything on it and greasy fries on the side. But that doesn't stop me from coming to Bea's house. In fact, I hate to admit that what she usually concocts, despite it being healthy, is delicious. This homemade hot chocolate with real whipped cream was no exception.

"That smells wonderful," I said, inhaling deeply. The chocolate smell gave the house a warm feeling that was the perfect contrast to the wind that was picking up outside.

Bea's cat, Peanut Butter, hopped up on the barstool next to me, and my hand instinctively reached out to pet her.

"Treacle was here." Peanut Butter had no problem interrupting my conversations with her thoughts. *"He said he'd be back, but I haven't seen him yet. It's getting bad outside. Do you think he's all right?"*

Since Bea was just telling me what she had used in the hot chocolate, I looked at the golden-yellow cat and scratched behind her ears.

"That Treacle knows where to keep safe. I'm sure he's fine. But he'll be staying in most of the time just as soon as we get our first snow, and that might be tonight. He always hates…"

My telepathic conversation was interrupted as the

front door quietly opened and shut. I looked up at Bea, who turned around and looked toward the front door.

"Jake?" she called.

There was no answer.

I got up from my stool and walked around the counter to stand next to Bea after scooping Peanut Butter up in my arms.

"Jake?"

"Yes, Bea. It's me." Jake sounded as if he wasn't really sure about that statement. Bea hustled around the counter and down the hallway, where I could hear a muffled conversation and then a gasp.

"Oh no!"

That sounded like bad news. At first I thought it had something to do with Jake's partner, Blake Samberg. I felt queasy as I waited for Bea and Jake to come into the kitchen.

"Cath is here," I could hear Bea say in reply to Jake's mumbles.

Before I could listen to any more, I heard a frantic scratching at the sliding glass back door.

"Treacle's back!" Peanut Butter announced.

I walked over to the door, flipped the lock, and pulled it open. Within a second of stepping into the warm house, he jumped up into my arms. He was shivering.

"My goodness, beastie," I said soothingly as I stroked the cat's cold fur. *"What happened?"*

"Nothing," Treacle said nervously. *"I just needed to get inside is all."*

"What? Was something chasing you?"

"Nothing I could see."

Obviously, I didn't care for the sound of that.

"Did you get into a fight with one of those other alley cats? Maybe they didn't like you slinking around their neighborhood."

"No." He jumped out of my arms and sat facing the glass door, looking out into the darkness. *"I just needed to get inside. I can't say I saw or heard or smelled anything. But I knew I needed to be home."*

"Okay." I bent down on one knee and looked out with my cat while scratching him behind the ears. *"Get warmed up, and after I have some hot chocolate, we'll head on home."*

"Alone?"

Just then, Bea and Jake walked into the kitchen.

"Hey, Jake." I waved. He looked pale, and his eyes were tired. "Bad day?"

"Hey, Cath. Yeah, you could say that." Jake was a really nice guy. He was like the brother I never had.

More importantly, he treated Bea really well. They were a bit of an odd couple, her being a witch who cooked vegetarian food and him being a police detective. But like the red and green colors of the season, they complemented each other. "We had to reinterview some of the kids from Bibich High School. It's an ugly situation all around."

"I was just making some hot chocolate for Cath and me. You want some, hon?" Bea asked, putting her hand on her husband's forearm as he leaned against the countertop like a cowboy at a saloon.

"That sounds good." He smiled, but it was obvious he was tired. "You know, at this time of year I should be hauling in guys who maybe just threw back one too many at their office parties, or maybe dealing with an accidental fire from too many Christmas lights on a dry Christmas tree. Not...child molestation."

"Crime never takes a holiday," Bea said as she stirred the delicious-smelling chocolate and poured the thick concoction into three coffee mugs.

"Neither does dry skin," I offered as I scratched my neck. "Can I ask you, Jake, do you have an opinion on Mr. Wayne? Do you think he did what those kids are saying?"

"I can't really tell." He wrapped his hands around

his mug and smiled up at Bea as she sprinkled shaved peppermint on top of the chocolate. "I think he's hiding something, but I'm just not sure it's what everyone thinks. But if I'm not careful, I might miss something. It's a real mess. And the guy is really up on his rights. He won't even ask to go to the bathroom unless he knows we've crossed every *T* and dotted every *I* because he's the kind of guy to catch us on a technicality if he can."

"There are a couple of kids, though, right?" I asked. "Are their stories the same?"

"Sort of," Jake said sadly. I could tell it was hurting him to talk about it. "But I don't make a call on it until I've seen everything and talked to everyone. I'm just not looking forward to that. Either the guy did it, and that's bad, or he didn't, and that might just be worse."

The thought hadn't occurred to me that maybe Mr. Wayne was innocent. Sad to say I am probably like most of the people in Wonder Falls who heard about the story and instantly assumed it could not be made up. I decided to follow Jake's lead and let everything fall into place before I gave my two cents' worth.

We sipped our hot chocolate, and I commented on Bea's beautiful Christmas decorations. She had her house tactfully decorated with ornaments and candles and small twinkling lights that gave the whole place a very grown-up, very mature and elegant feel. It suited her.

Aunt Astrid's house was covered with over sixty years of collecting and buying and, well, hoarding all kinds of trinkets and tassels. Stepping into her house at Christmastime was like time travel back to my childhood. Even with my parents gone, I couldn't help but always feel the warmth and love stepping in the front door. Sure, I wished my parents, especially my mother, could be around. But they aren't. My aunt Astrid and Bea are. Through all the years, they have made sure no boogeyman from underneath the bed has ever come to take me, as it did my mother. I feel safe and warm when I am with them.

"Well, I think I've had enough hot chocolate for tonight." I stood and stretched. I slipped on my coat and gave Jake a kiss on the cheek. "Get some rest. You're starting to look your age."

"Thanks, Cath. You smell," he teased back.

"Oh, what about what Mom said?" Bea's eyes widened.

"I think you could just watch from your door that I make it home," I offered. I didn't want to be a thorn in Jake's side, especially after him having such a bad day. "Besides, I've got Treacle. We'll be fine."

"Okay, but flip your porch light when you are safe inside," Bea ordered as she walked my cat and me to the door. "Treacle, make sure Cath doesn't get in any trouble." She scratched him behind his ears then kissed me on the cheek.

"I'll see you tomorrow at work," I assured Bea as I stepped outside and began my short journey across the street. I thought about my decorations in my house and was looking forward to getting home. My Christmas tree was small but was loaded with secondhand ornaments I'd bought at the thrift store. Nothing matched, and gold and silver tinsel covered just about every surface, hung around every picture, door, and window frame, and the tackier the lights, the better. My tree was covered with two strands of lights that were three hundred bulbs each. It almost lit up my whole house.

But before I could get inside my house, the snow started to come down. I turned and thought I saw Bea standing in her doorway, waving. I waved back and pulled my coat tighter around me, but when I looked in the direction of my house, I couldn't see it. It was just snow. A great wall of falling snow.

"Treacle?" I looked down and saw the black fur

being almost completely devoured in the white precipitation. "Treacle!" I reached down and pulled him up by the scruff of his neck as if he were my kitten. "What is this?"

"I don't know. But there's a cat around here." I felt Treacle's body go rigid in my arms. He was staring off down the street, and he didn't blink. I looked and didn't see anything. But I heard it. The familiar low growl of a cat that was not happy.

My porch light was getting dimmer, and I was afraid that if I didn't get to it right away, we'd never see the light of day again. Squeezing Treacle to my chest, I trudged toward the light. The snow was at my ankles, then my calves, then my knees within seconds. How could this be?

The growling sound was even closer. I couldn't see where it was coming from, but I was sure I could feel the heat of its breath cutting through the cold, icy snowflakes, and I bolted. Hiking my legs up as the snow reached my thighs, I ran as best I could to what I hoped was my front porch. I was so disoriented that I wasn't sure anymore. But there was a light, and it was getting closer, so I held on to Treacle and lumbered as fast as I could. Finally, I fell onto my cement sidewalk, nearly smooshing Treacle in the process.

"Thank God for Aunt Astrid's protection spells on our houses. Are you okay?" I asked him.

"What was that?" He leapt from my arms and circled along the sidewalk, looking back in the direction we had come.

Remembering the growl, I jumped up and whirled around, only to face my yard. A slight dusting of snow fell to the ground, barely enough to make a snow angel, let alone the blizzard I was sure I'd just fallen out of.

"I don't know," I whispered. Quickly, I pulled my keys from my pocket, unlocked the front door, scooted Treacle inside, shut and locked the doors behind me, and then flicked my lights for Bea. I peeked out the window to see her flickering hers back. That was our code that we were home and safe. "But whatever it was, I don't think Bea saw it. That's it for tonight, kitty. You're staying in."

"You won't get an argument from me." He rubbed his body along my leg then trotted off for a drink of water. I did the same.

The night went by quietly with no other strange incidents. It wasn't until I saw the tracks in the frost the next morning that I felt a chill race over me.

"I told you there was a cat out here," Treacle said as he came outside with me to walk to the café.

Maybe it was a cat. But the prints were about the size of car tires, and it looked as though they were dragging something alongside them. Before I could study them, the sun made quick work of the frost, and everything melted away.

Greek Tragedies

❧❦❧

"I could count how many snowflakes I saw fall last night on one hand." Bea shook her head as she listened to my story. "But I will admit that I blacked out for a flash of time."

"What do you mean?" Aunt Astrid asked. She was at her table with a deck of tarot cards for any emergency readings that might be requested from our customers.

"Well, I was watching Cath cross the street and…"

"Didn't I tell you to have Jake and you walk her home?"

"Busted," I muttered. "Aunt Astrid, it was my fault. Jake looked so tired that I didn't want to make him bundle himself up to walk me just across the street and…"

"*And* when I tell you to do something, you do it!" Aunt Astrid yelled. I don't think I have heard Aunt Astrid yell at Bea and me since we were in the ninth grade and tried to conjure a spitting demon to attack Darla Castellano, who was, and still is, my nemesis. We didn't realize spitting demons multiplied like gremlins if a person screamed. And a person *always* screamed.

"Yes, ma'am." I felt horrible. "Sorry."

"I'm sorry, too, Mom."

My aunt glared at us. A few bubbly older ladies came bustling into the café, setting off the bells over the door. It was obvious that they had been shopping, as they each had a handful of bags in their hands. Two coffees and two chocolate-and-raspberry scones with a sprinkling of peppermint candy cane over the top, and they were happily talking at a corner table, oblivious to the tension between us Greenstones.

"There is something out there," Aunt Astrid rumbled. "It gets darker earlier this time of year, and whatever it is, it's using that to its advantage. Now you both better tell me exactly what you did last night, and don't leave anything out."

I swallowed as if I were about to be grounded for not only sneaking out with a boy, but for smoking a

43

cigarette, too. Bea and I told Aunt Astrid everything. I started with the snowstorm, and Bea ended by saying she had watched me cross the street but had fallen asleep standing up.

"I didn't think anything of it because when I snapped to, Cath was flipping her porch light on and off that she'd made it home. I just chalked it up to being tired."

Aunt Astrid pulled out a sheet of paper from her pants pocket. It was wrinkled, and from what I could see, it had scribbled notes all over it. She wrote down a couple of things then folded it and put it in her pocket.

"You girls." She sighed. "What would I do if anything happened to either one of you?"

Bea and I had no idea what Aunt Astrid was talking about, but she was making both of us very nervous.

"Mom?" Bea stepped up first. "What is this all about?"

"I'm not sure." Aunt Astrid smiled and put her hand to her daughter's cheek. "But promise me that if I ask you to do something, you girls will *do it*!"

"I promise," I answered quickly. I didn't want any more trouble, and the last thing I wanted was my aunt mad at me.

"Me, too." Bea crossed her heart.

Aunt Astrid let out a big sigh and smiled at us.

"Good. Now that we have that out of the way. Cath?" I held my breath. I wasn't sure what she was going to reveal, and I wasn't sure I was prepared. "Don't you have a date with Tom tonight?"

I slapped my forehead.

"Yikes! I forgot." What kind of girlfriend was I? In the history of girlfriends, there has never been one who would forget her date with a blue-eyed, black-haired, cowboy-boot-wearing Romeo like Tom except me.

"Where are you two going tonight?"

"Thankfully, he said it was casual, so I can wear what I'm wearing now." I inspected my reflection in the toaster on the counter and shrugged.

"You look lovely," Bea assured me. "Navy blue complements your complexion and brings out your eyes."

I tugged at the blue Christmas sweater I was wearing. It was from my collection of ugly sweaters for the holiday season and had giant white snowflakes knitted throughout with silver and gold gems bedazzled onto the center of each one.

"Is he picking you up here?" Aunt Astrid asked.

"Yeah. Around seven, if I remember right." I scratched my head.

"Okay. I will put a protection spell on the both of you. He won't even notice I'm doing it. The same goes for you, young lady." Aunt Astrid pointed at Bea.

"Can you tell us what we're up against? I mean, usually we're pretty strong together, and you seem to be flying solo on this one," I interrupted.

My aunt slipped her arms through Bea's and mine and pulled us close to her. She smiled, but there was something scaring her, and that scared both of us.

"Truthfully, I am not trusting my own sight," she said. "I am afraid that my powers just aren't what they used to be. There is something out there. I can feel it. I can hear it. I think at times I can even smell it. But I can't see it, and I'm afraid of the reason why."

"What would be that reason, Mom?" Bea lost all the pink in her cheeks.

"My time is coming." Aunt Astrid straightened her back and blinked back tears.

There was a story in those Greek tragedies of a soothsayer that could see everything coming but not the day of his own demise. I wondered if knowing or not knowing was better. Right now, I wished I didn't know this.

"I don't need to go out tonight, Aunt Astrid," I said. "We can stay at the house and figure things out and then…"

"You most certainly do need to go out tonight." She flipped her long, wild hair behind her. It was still pale blond with streaks of grey. Her body didn't appear to be degenerating in any obvious way, and she didn't complain about her joints or her hips or her hands, as some people her age might. "When a handsome man wants to take you someplace, you go. Now, enough of this negative business. As I said, I'll put a protection spell on the both of you, and we'll go on living as we always have, as a family."

"M-Mama?" Bea took her mom's hands, and I could see she was trying to find something, anything that she could fix, unblock, release, or tighten that would explain why her mother had said she was afraid she was losing her sight. But there wasn't anything there. Bea bit her lip.

"Come on now. We're at work. We've got customers. It's Christmastime." My aunt took each of our hands and squeezed them tight. "And I'm not licked yet." She winked.

It was true that keeping busy and doing your job

well could make you feel a whole lot better when you were down. In fact, Aunt Astrid, Bea and I had a rather jolly time at the café. Bea told us about the worst present Jake had ever bought for her when they first got married.

"A garlic press?" I laughed. "And what else?"

"Nothing!" she wailed, laughing until tears came out of the corners of her eyes. "He thought it would be what I wanted since I complained that my hands would smell like garlic when I crushed it and cut it with a knife. He didn't know how much garlic can be used in magic and that using a press would ruin the spell."

For some reason, that detail made the story that much funnier. We held our sides, we were laughing so hard. By the time seven rolled around and Tom showed up, I was sure he thought we were drunk.

"Have a good time, you two," Aunt Astrid said after casually and discreetly putting a protection spell over us. I kissed her and Bea on the cheek before stepping out into the brisk night air with Tom. I felt his warm hand take hold of mine.

"So where are we headed?" I asked, inhaling the wonderful smell of logs burning in a fireplace.

"Bibich High School," he chirped.

"What? Why?" I was shocked. Surely he knew

what was going on there. What could possibly be the reason for going there?

"Because it is a home game for the football team, and with all the trouble they've been having, it's important to show them support at a time like this." He smiled.

"I don't think I've ever been to a high school football game," I muttered. "Not even when I was in high school. Okay. What's in it for me?"

Tom chuckled and squeezed my hand.

"Oh, I think you'll be pleasantly surprised. They've got hot dogs, nachos with cheese, slices of cheese pizza."

"You had me at hot dogs." I smiled happily.

When we got to the Bibich football field, we were just in time for kickoff. The place was packed, and there was so much team spirit that you could cut it with a knife. Everyone was bundled up and cheering madly as the players took the field.

"Hot dog?" Tom asked after we had found a seat on the aluminum bleachers.

"And nachos, and pizza, and a can of pop."

"Coming right up." He bounded down the steps as if he had been doing this every day for the past year. I suffered slightly from vertigo and was happy we weren't up too high.

It was a beautiful night without a cloud in the sky. I peeked around to see if there was anyone I might know, but not surprisingly, I saw a sea of strangers. As I took in the sight of the field, the opposing team's colors, and the cheerleaders wearing sweatshirts and turtlenecks while still having bare legs, I came across a set of eyes that were definitely trained on me. He smiled.

Now, I'm not going to be falsely modest. I'm not ugly. I'm certainly no beauty like Bea, but my curves are in all the right places. But there was no way this handsome man could have known that since I was wearing a long coat and he was all the way down in the bleachers closer to the field. I didn't smile back. Instead I searched for Tom and finally spotted him chatting with a couple of guys before he headed back my way with half a cardboard box filled with food.

Before I could say anything, the loudspeaker interrupted.

"Ladies and gentlemen. We'd like to take this time to welcome the newest addition to the Bibich High School faculty. Mr. Hank Tumble!"

I watched as the students went absolutely crazy, clapping and cheering. To get teenagers to do anything other than sulk or complain was a huge accomplishment. The same guy who had been smiling at me just a short while earlier stood up and waved around to the crowd as some of the kids around him patted him on the back and whooped even louder. Once again, his eyes scanned the crowd and found me. He was good-looking in a perfect, male-model way. He waved and smiled broadly.

"Do you know that man?" Tom asked as he sat down.

"Never saw him before in my life," I admitted.

"Well, he sure looks like he wants to get to know you."

I rolled my eyes and looked at Tom.

"Please don't tell me you're jealous." I sighed.

"Me? Jealous?" Tom took his seat next to me. "Not at all. I knew I'd be in for some competition sooner or later. I'm ready for it." He clapped his hands and rubbed them together as if he were getting ready to start chopping wood or pulling boulders out of the ground with his bare hands or some other manly task.

Mr. Tumble continued to look in my direction for several more seconds until he finally sat down.

"I got a large pop. I wouldn't have been able to carry another one. I hope you don't mind if we share." He grinned as he handed me the box.

"I don't have cooties," I replied. "Soft pretzels, too? This is the best dinner ever."

Tom scooted closer. We cozied up together, and once again I found myself forgetting about everything else, like Aunt Astrid and the weird snowstorm from last night. It wasn't until Bibich High School scored their first touchdown that the conversation became much more serious.

"It looks like the whole town had the same idea as us. I've never seen a high school game this packed," Tom said as he unwrapped the silver tinfoil around his second hot dog. "It's nice to see everyone getting together to make sure the kids feel their support."

"I agree." I scooped some nacho cheese on a chip and shoveled it into my mouth. There was nothing quite like hot nacho cheese on a cold winter evening. "It's really a shame about that boy going missing. My family and I know his mother. She's so sad. It's heartbreaking."

"You mean girl."

"What?"

"It's a girl that's gone missing. Her name is Donna."

"No." I shook my head. "Bruce Lyle has been missing for over a week now. His mother said he had been having some trouble at school with some kids and he was also part of the group that accused Mr. Wayne of *that stuff*," I whispered.

"What are you talking about?" Tom asked. "The girl, Donna Flint, went missing about three days ago."

"I'm just telling you what I heard. From the police and from the boy's mother as well." I felt as if I should apologize, but Tom put his hand on my arm and looked me square in the eyes. "Bruce Lyle Jr. has been missing for over a week. Just up and disappeared."

"You're sure a boy went missing?" he asked.

"One hundred percent."

"It's got to be because I am Unincorporated Wonder Falls and you guys are Wonder Falls. Our fire and police and waterworks and road construction are all separate, even though technically we should all be under one umbrella." Tom rubbed his chin. "I need to talk to your police department. If there have been two disappearances, we've got a serious problem on our hands."

Runaway

✤

In between the downs and the passes and the fouls and the touchdowns—the last of which there was only one from the opposing team— Tom and I talked quietly about the two teens who went missing.

Donna Flint was a sophomore and had just broken up with her boyfriend.

"From what her parents told us, she was not an especially troubled girl," Tom said. "Just the normal teenage angst. Everything was a drama, but she had good grades, and no one seemed to have anything really negative to say about her. She wasn't popular, but she wasn't unpopular, either."

"Breaking up with a boyfriend can be hard," I offered. For some reason, the image of Blake Samberg popped into my head, and I felt a sharp twang in my chest. For sure I thought Tom could read my expression, and I prayed he wouldn't ask me about it. "Especially if it was her first serious boyfriend."

"From what her mom said, she had been the one to do the breaking up."

"I'm assuming you checked the boy out? Teenage angst and all?" I shook my head, thinking of how cruel and selfish teenagers could be.

"We did, and he was upset but not enough to harm anyone." Tom lifted his eyebrows. "Besides, he was lanky and on the short side. Donna could have probably held her own in a fight. Plus, he was with his parents at the movies the night she disappeared. I didn't get the vibe the ex-boyfriend was anything more than that. Just an ex-boyfriend."

Tom said Donna was supposed to go to her job at a burger place after school but never showed up. They checked with her boss, who said she was a responsible employee and got along well with everyone.

"How did she get to her job?" I asked.

"She walked. It was only about five blocks from her house," Tom answered. "It really is like she vanished."

"Runaway is out of the question?" I leaned closer

to Tom. "Bruce Lyle's mom said that he was gone but that none of his clothes were missing. No coat. No shoes, even. It was like he was just plucked up and taken away as is."

"Donna just had what she wore to school that day and her book bag. Nothing more." Tom sighed. "How about some more nachos?"

"Soft pretzel?" I asked. As crazy as it may seem, I'd had enough nachos. Tom gave me a wink that made me blush. He stood and made his way down to the concession stand.

Bibich was losing by one touchdown, but it didn't seem to be dampening the spirits of everyone in attendance. I looked around and saw the groups of teenage cliques and chatting parents and thought nothing had changed since the days when I went to high school.

As I adjusted my scarf, I saw that Mr. Tumble was again looking in my direction. In return for eye contact, I got a wave and grin as though I had invited him to dinner or something. It was a little unnerving. There was something about this Mr. Tumble that rubbed me the wrong way. He wasn't ugly, and he certainly hadn't done anything to make me cringe or clutch my pearls, but there was something in his dark eyes that flashed every so often that made me think of the eyes of a cobra.

"Sorry, they are all out of pretzels." Tom flopped down next to me.

"That's okay." I patted him on the knee. "How about we go to the café for a nightcap?"

He nodded and smiled. As he took my hand and led me carefully down the bleachers, I kept an eye on Mr. Tumble. He was watching us with that same grin on his face.

The kids around him were talking and asking him questions. He was completely accepted by the young crowd, but I could tell that he was more absorbed by Tom and me walking out of the football game. I'm not sure how far he watched, but I will say that I didn't feel out of his range until we were completely out of the parking lot and heading toward the café.

"So what do you think Bruce and Donna had in common?" I asked as Tom drove. The sound of my own voice startled me.

"That's a good question," he mumbled. "Right now, all we know is that they go to the same school."

"I wonder if they had any of the same classes," I offered. "Bruce's mother said he was one of the children involved in the scandal with Mr. Wayne."

Tom slowed the truck for a second. "The Flints

said the same thing. They said that he had made inappropriate comments to her but that it had never progressed to anything further than that."

"My gosh." I was used to seeing monsters and ghouls, but to be part of an investigation where the culprit was your average, run-of-the-mill pervert was a totally different ballgame for me. "That's definitely a commonality, don't you think?"

"Yes." Tom gripped the steering wheel tightly as he drove. "The parents didn't make a big issue of it. I don't know what Bruce's experience with the man was, but if it was something big, Mr. Wayne would be in even hotter water. It might've been worth it to silence the boy."

"You don't think he took those kids?"

"A desperate man will do desperate things." Tom would know better than I. "If he was confused about the roles of teachers to children, then heaven knows what he thought he should do in the face of possible arrest and charges being brought."

"My gosh. I don't mean to sound so Pollyanna-ish, but the guy had to do this at Christmastime? It isn't enough he has hurt these kids but now has to seek revenge during the holidays when families are together the most. It makes me sick."

"Well, the guy is innocent until proven guilty."

"Yikes!" I had completely forgotten about the incident at the Brew-Ha-Ha and quickly filled Tom in on the details.

We finally pulled up in front of the café just as Aunt Astrid and Bea were cleaning up for the night.

"Can you spare us a leftover brownie or maybe some of that chocolate fudge Kevin made this morning?" I smiled, leaning over the counter. "I was just telling Tom about what happened the other day with Mr. Mavery and Mr. Wayne."

"What an ordeal," Aunt Astrid exclaimed.

"It was re-donk-u-lous," Bea added as she served up two tiny one-inch squares of fudge on a tiny teacup saucer. "Enjoy."

"If that's how the adults are acting, we aren't going to get anywhere with them." Tom looked at us. "I hate to say this, but the kids probably have more answers than any of us on the police department—either department—put together. Bea, do you think Jake would talk to me about this?"

"I know he would," Bea replied. "I'll tell him to expect you to drop by the precinct tomorrow if that works for you."

"Tell him I'll be there first thing. Thanks, Bea." He popped the square of fudge in his mouth but within seconds was regretting that decision.

"Unless you have teeth made of one-hundred-percent sugar, usually you just nibble chocolate this rich." I laughed. I had to. He was working his jaw like a dog that had stolen a lick of peanut butter.

After a few more minutes of small talk, Tom offered to drive me home. Aunt Astrid and Bea were leaving together, so I waved good-bye. As soon as I got in the car, Tom asked me about the Policemen's Christmas Ball.

"Have you got a dress?"

"I have something in mind," I lied. I hadn't been able to pick out a Christmas present for Tom, nor had I been able to find a dress that I liked for this fancy, formal affair. Now, with this disappearance of two kids, I was afraid Christmas was going to be shanghaied by the Ghost of Indecision.

"Maybe I could come in and you could show it to me," he said innocently but with a naughty smirk.

"I think you are just going to have to wait. I still need to find the right accessories and shoes and things."

"All right. But I won't wait for this." He leaned in and kissed me on the lips. I would have liked to stay there in his warm truck, pretending we were teenagers ourselves, but I was too distracted to fully enjoy myself. I kept thinking about those two missing teens.

They had Mr. Wayne in common. He was out on bail, and they were now missing. That looked pretty suspicious, but of course, the police couldn't just lock him up with no evidence.

"I think I better go in before you lead me down the path of scandal and destruction." I eased away from Tom, who held my hands tightly.

"I don't need to tell you how crazy I am about you, do I, Cath?"

"Maybe you don't *need* to," I said. "But it's nice to hear."

He scooted closer to me again.

"I'm crazy about you, Cath." He kissed my cheek. "Really crazy about you." Then he kissed my other cheek. "So much so I don't even want to think of a day I don't see you even for just a few minutes."

"I'm glad to hear that," I replied. "Would you carry my books home from school tomorrow?"

"I'll stop by the café after I talk with Jake."

I nodded and gave Tom a full kiss on the lips before hopping out of the truck and giddily shuffling to the front door.

"*You're late.*" Treacle looked at me sternly from the

edge of my small foyer before he busied himself licking his paw.

I shut the door and locked the dead bolt.

"Late?" I peeled off my coat and hung it up so I could pick up Treacle. "Late for what?"

"Late to let me out for an hour or two." Treacle looked at me seriously.

"I'll let you out now. Just be back in an hour, and I'll…"

"I'm not going out into the dark."

"What?" I was shocked. Treacle not going out at night was like me turning down a cheeseburger. It never happened. "Why not?"

"There's a cat out there."

"So? You've dealt with some of those ornery cats before. I know you can handle yourself."

"No. There's a cat out there I haven't seen yet." Treacle purred against me. *"I'll wait until morning to go out."*

"Okay, big kitty. You stay with me." This was unusual, for sure. I knew Treacle, and he rarely, if ever, backed down from a confrontation with another cat. Sometimes he'd win the turf war, and the extra few feet of territory would be his to roam freely on. Sometimes he'd lose and be missing a piece of his ear or a clump of hair from his tail. Either way, he never backed down due to the size or attitude of the opposing cat. This beast must have been a bit meaner and larger than Treacle had been used to.

"There is nothing wrong with walking away from a fight," I said encouragingly.

"*Or running away?*" he asked with a serious tint to his eyes making them an even more opaque green.

"Yes, honey. It's okay to run away from a fight at times, too." He didn't seem to want to talk about it anymore, so I didn't push it. I assured him he could go out in the morning if he liked or even come with me to the café.

"*The café sounds good.*"

"Then it's a date, handsome."

Spiderwebs

T he next day as Treacle and I stepped outside and walked across the street to Bea's house, I had the feeling something was going to happen.

"Do you feel that?" I asked Bea as we walked down the sidewalk. When the weather was nice, we preferred to walk to the café. Today was cold, and we were bundled up in scarves and earmuffs and gloves, but the sun was shining, and there was no breeze of any kind. Not even the slightest rustle of the trees.

"I don't feel anything," Bea admitted, looking at me then tilting her head as if she were listening. "Nope. Just seems like a regular morning to me. Maybe it's...no. I won't say it."

"Say what?"

"Maybe it's...I don't know... the feeling of love?"

Bea swung her hips with her steps and pouted her lips. "You did seem extra calm last night when you guys stopped in the café. Relaxed, even. That isn't your usual modus operandi."

"You are off your rocker."

"Well, if you aren't, then I sure do feel sorry for Tom because he is totally smitten with you, and I'd hate to see such a fine-looking man with such a good head on his shoulders go to waste."

"Nobody's going to waste. We aren't at the love stage yet. Come on. It's been just a handful of months, and you know these things take time. How long did it take you to know Jake was the one?"

"Not long. But I'm not talking about Jake and me; I'm talking about you and Officer Thomas Warner." Bea slipped her arm through mine and squeezed it. "I'm just happy to see you happy. Let's be honest, I know you had feelings for Blake, maybe still do a little, but he just didn't move fast enough. That's what I told him when he asked about you and..."

"Blake asked about me?" I was slightly embarrassed by my blatant interest. I really wished that I could shrug it off. I knew for a fact that Darla Castellano, that bad girl from my past, would've been able to move on without looking back even once. Of course, she had a heart of stone, ice in her veins, and probably several demonic voices in her head, so that might be a contributing factor. But I wasn't like that. I wanted to know.

"Well, yeah." Bea hawed. "He was just asking if things were getting serious with Tom and stuff."

"And what did you tell him?" I squeezed her arm.

"I said that I thought Tom was treating you the way you should be treated and that it takes a special guy to crack the crusty, scaly, barnacle-like shell that you reside beneath."

"As long as you said that, I'm good with it." I chuckled.

"Yeah, well, it's too late now, isn't it?" Bea laughed.

But both of us stopped the second we saw the front door to the Brew-Ha-Ha. Giant spiderwebs of cracked glass spread from top to bottom. The fact that the metal frame was still intact was a miracle.

"What in the world?" I yelled.

"Really?" Bea groaned. "Vandalizing at Christmas? What is the world coming to? My mom is going to be so mad."

"Wait a minute." I held Bea back for a second. "Is that blood on there?" I pointed to a corner of the glass near the bottom of the door that was no longer red but caked with a dry, rusty-brown substance.

"Someone's in there," Bea hissed and pointed to movement behind the counter. "Mom?"

Both of our hands were trembling as we tried to unlock the door, but it wouldn't budge. Bea immediately called Jake while I ordered Treacle to stay with Bea.

I ran around to the rear of the café to try and get in through the back door. The dumpster had been pushed in front of it.

The putrid smell made my face crinkle. I swallowed hard as I grabbed the dirty handle of the dumpster, pulling with all my strength.

The tiny wheels reluctantly began to swivel and roll enough distance for me to squeeze behind the massive green blockade.

I yanked the door open and dashed inside.

"Aunt Astrid!" I found her crouched behind the counter. "Wait, let me get Bea in here."

Standing on weak legs and with trembling hands, I unlocked the damaged front door. Bea raced up to her mother with tears streaming down her face.

"Mom?" She took her hand. "Mama. Can you hear me?"

"Bea. Cath." Aunt Astrid managed a smile. "Yes. I can hear you just fine. Help me up."

"No. Don't move," Bea insisted. "Wait until the

paramedics get here." I stood back and watched as Bea held onto her mother. She felt along her arms and legs and placed her hand gently over her mother's heart, breathing with her and asking Aunt Astrid whether there was pain or if she felt any discomfort.

Bea's healing was a little different from what the EMTs would do. She cried with relief to find her mother's emotional skeleton was still very much intact. But when she looked at her mother's knees, she began to cry.

"Mama." She sobbed. "What happened?"

"After you left with Jake, I went down into the bunker."

"Wait, you were here alone?" My own eyes filled with tears, and I could tell by Bea's reaction that she was thinking the exact same thing I was. "What about all that talk about us sticking together and not being alone, and here you are going against your own advice."

"I found it." Aunt Astrid clutched Bea's hand tightly. "The disturbance, the ripple I've been seeing. I found something in the books that might explain it."

"That's just fine, young lady, but it doesn't explain what went on here."

I could hear the sirens and knew that if Bea had

called Jake, he was probably several blocks ahead of them. If my aunt was going to explain this whole thing, she had better start talking.

"When I came upstairs, I thought I heard a cat." She pointed toward the door. "It was dark, and I knew the temperature had dropped. I couldn't imagine an animal being out there, so I cracked the door."

Bea took her hand, and I looked out the window, hoping Jake wouldn't arrive until after she finished her story.

"What was out there?" Bea asked.

"At first I thought it was just the wind kicking up some flurries. But then I saw the eyes. They were huge." Aunt Astrid trembled.

Just then, Jake's car came skidding to a stop outside the café. Leaving the engine running, he took one look at the door and gasped. He barged in. His eyes were wild with worry. Blake was not far behind him as he stepped out of the passenger side.

"Where is she?" Jake wheezed.

I pointed behind the counter. No words would come out of my mouth. No coherent thought would form in my mind. I was just standing there like a chump waiting for someone, anyone, to tell me what to do.

Blake walked in wearing that same jacket and tie he seemed to always wear. He looked at me as if he hated himself for not having gotten there sooner or for not having the right comment to say. He looked around the café, at the door and the floor and the windows as he made his way to my side.

I was prepared for him to ask some serious questions about what exactly happened or what we saw, but he didn't. Instead, what he said made me cry.

"Thank God you're okay."

That was it. That was all it took, and Niagara Falls fell from my eyes. I don't know why I started crying. My aunt was okay. She was talking, and if these guys had given us just a few seconds more, we wouldn't have to wait to find out what happened to her. I let Blake put his arms around me, and I leaned into him, staining the lapel of his suit with my tears.

When I pulled away, I saw a familiar red pickup truck pull up behind Jake's car, just a second before the ambulance arrived from the opposite direction. Without thinking, I pulled away from Blake and ran to Tom.

Tom held me close and whispered, "What happened?"

I couldn't help but spill everything I knew up to

that point, including that Aunt Astrid had been working late.

"Jake and Blake and you and the paramedics all showed up. She didn't finish the story. I don't know what happened. I don't know what broke the door or why." I slipped my hand into Tom's. "But I'm really glad you are here."

"I had said I was going to meet Jake first thing. I was talking about the disappearances of those kids when Bea called." He squeezed my hand and began walking toward the café entrance. "Come on. Let's see what we can find out."

I nodded and was happy Tom was there to make the next few decisions for me. When we stepped inside, Aunt Astrid was arguing with the EMTs.

"I said I'm fine. I just lost my balance and scraped up my knees. Then that poor bird flew right into the door. I just had a dilly of a night."

"Mom. Don't you want to go to the hospital just to get checked out?" Bea pleaded, looking at her husband. "Maybe you need to stay there overnight, just to be safe."

"No, Bea. Really, I scraped my knees on the steps up from the bunker. That's all. I didn't hit my head or anything, so I don't know why you think I need to stay overnight." Aunt Astrid dusted off her blouse. "I spent the night here. I'd like to be in my own bed tonight. Thanks."

"It's just to make sure," Bea said.

"No, and that's final." Aunt Astrid was determined not to get into that ambulance. Frankly, I was relieved. She was her old fiery self, and whether or not she had the right to refuse medical attention, I wasn't sure, but I did love hearing her argue. "I'm still your mother. And yours, too." She scoffed at Jake. "I'm fine. Now just spray a little Bactine on these scrapes, slap on some Band-Aids, and let's get these doors open for business."

The EMTs chuckled and did as Aunt Astrid asked. Within minutes, Jake had the plywood guys over to put up temporary plywood where the glass door used to be.

"What is all this around the door?" Jake asked, looking down.

"I was bringing up a bag of salt for Kevin last night. I dropped it when I was startled. That's all."

Bea and I hadn't even noticed the salt. But it was not only spilled across the threshold of the door, but along all the windows as well. No one noticed. No one but Bea and I, and we knew all too well what the salt was for. Apparently, it worked to keep whatever it was out, at least for now.

With everyone still hanging around and the morning rush quickly approaching, Aunt Astrid wasn't going to have any time to tell us what was out there last night. They didn't seem to be in any hurry to leave.

Jake and Tom continued the conversation that had obviously been interrupted when Bea called this morning. The strange thing was that Blake was talking with my aunt. From what I could see, he wasn't taking notes. Surprisingly, he was doing most of the talking. His head was down, and as he spoke, he looked at the floor, but when my aunt replied, he looked directly into her eyes. What were they talking about?

Wrinkled Thing

❧

"Hey, Bea," I whispered. "Do you have any idea what your mom and Blake are talking about?"

"Probably you."

"What?" I yelped, grabbing everyone's attention and pulling it toward my bright-red face.

"Well, yeah." She pulled me by my sleeve to turn my back to the group so no one could see our lips moving and possibly decipher this top-secret conversation. "He's had those sad-puppy-dog eyes since you started dating Tom. But that's often how things go. Nobody knows what they've got until it's gone."

"But he never had me," I whispered back, pulling my lips down in thought. "He started dating Darla Castellano. AKA the Devil."

"It doesn't matter with a man." Bea took the

dustpan and bent down while I swept. "He can sing the blues to Aunt Astrid all he wants, and she will give him sound advice. But that advice might be to just move along."

Those words gripped the inside of my chest. Was that what I wanted? Did I want him gone and moved along? I couldn't think straight. Not now.

Kevin Baker, our culinary creative genius, arrived holding a paper bag full of fresh herbs and some fruit. He stood at the back door by the kitchen with his mouth hanging open. It didn't take long for us to get him up to speed—the parts that we could tell him, anyway.

"No worries, ladies. I'll handle the kitchen."

I think that was the most I'd heard him say in my presence. I liked Kevin. He was quiet and kind and came up with some of the most amazing treats, and if he ever decided to leave and open his own café, I would follow his double white-and-dark-chocolate truffles anywhere. Now I was getting hungry.

"Astrid, I'm going to come by tonight and pick you and Bea up and drive you home," Jake said. "No arguing. I don't care what needs to get done. You are coming with me, and I'm walking you up your porch and not leaving until I hear the dead bolt click on the other side of the door."

"Fine. Fine." My aunt waved her hand as if she were waving a hankie at a departing ship.

Blake walked over to me. Bea made like a banana and split, quickly going over to her mother.

"Do you need a lift home, Cath?"

"Cath. I'll do the same," Tom yelled as he and Jake stepped to the new plywood door. "We'll get something to eat, and I'll bring you home."

"Okay." I smiled. But when I looked up at Blake, I saw frustration there. I didn't like this. Some girls would be tickled pink to have two fellows engaged in a machismo contest over them, but this wasn't for me. It was awkward and embarrassing, and to be honest, it was cruel. I didn't like to see Blake like this. I didn't like to see him in second place.

"But he didn't mind how you felt when you saw him with Darla."

I heard the familiar voice in my head and looked to see Treacle on the table, comfortably splayed out with his back feet and tail dangling off the edge.

"And here I thought I was giving myself that great advice," I told him.

I looked back up at Blake and smiled as I reached out and gently patted his arm.

"Thanks, Blake. Tom will take me."

What made this even worse was that Blake

nodded with class and dignity. He walked over to Tom and Jake as if they were all just good old chums who would probably be meeting up this weekend for beer and paintball. I'll never understand men.

Finally, the EMTs, Jake, Blake, and Tom were gone. Kevin was in the kitchen, and we could hear the soft sound of his radio playing back there as he bustled about in his own world in order to make ours a little sweeter.

"So?" I pulled out the chair at my aunt's favorite table and motioned for her to sit. "Are you going to tell us what you saw or what?"

She nodded and carefully eased into her seat. Bea and I both saw her wince as her knees ached.

"Mom—" Bea started but was quickly interrupted.

"I'm all right, Bea." Her sharp blue eyes darted back and forth between us. "For now. For now, we are all right. But I'm afraid if we don't get a handle on what is in this town, there will be more missing children."

"Children?" I mumbled.

"As I was saying. I thought I heard a cat." Aunt Astrid walked to the door and looked out onto the street. "I didn't see anything and thought it might be hurt. So I unlocked the door and stepped outside. I walked out to the sidewalk, then I stepped to the edge of the street. Had I taken one more step, I fear I would have been too far from the front door to have made it back inside."

She pulled her sleeves down at the cuffs.

"At first there were just eyes. They reflected the light as if they were sucking all of it in, making the street darker. I tried to see if this dimension had crossed with another, putting us in the same space for a short while. Sort of like what happens when people spot Bigfoot. But it was here. It was in this dimension, and it had no intention of leaving."

I sat down on one of the stools at the counter. Bea handed me a stack of napkins and some plastic silverware to start rolling together for our takeout orders. She got the coffee started as we listened.

"It got bigger as I watched the eyes sink into soft, fleshy sockets. The creature, which had sounded like a kitten in trouble, meowed in front of me. Like it was so proud of the joke it had played to get me outside. How that delicate, harmless little voice could crawl from the throat of the beast that was forming in front of my very eyes, I don't know."

"What was it?" Bea whispered.

"It was a cat, all right. A hairless, wrinkled thing that sprouted jagged, broken claws on each paw. Its snout was pulled back in a grimace, baring two rows of sharp teeth, and its tail, if you want to call it a tail, was more like a hardened, dried leather whip."

I looked at Treacle, who was sitting up on the table and staring outside.

"Its body was draped in that same wrinkled skin, except for the haunches, which seemed unnaturally bloated. Despite having no hair, it didn't seem to mind the cold. Steam billowed from its open maw, and as I stared, I saw it slowly pulling one thick leg tighter underneath itself. It was getting ready to pounce."

"Aunt Astrid, does this thing have a name?"

"I tried to find out. As fast as I could, I turned and ran, but I got tangled over my own feet. That's what caused the scuffs." She tapped both of her bandaged knees and shook her head. "But I was up and running faster than I ever imagined. I mean, these old bones didn't fail me. As soon as my hand gripped the handle, I swear I could feel its breath on the back of my neck. Once I was across the threshold, I yanked the door shut and snapped the dead bolt. When I looked up, it slammed headfirst into the glass."

My aunt stopped for a moment and shook her head.

"I knew there was something in Wonder Falls that was causing a disturbance. I could see ripples of it. I felt the presence, but it was disguised as uneasiness, like an electric hum from a transformer or something. You know it's there, and it bothers you, but you can't quite find the source, and even if you did, how would you stop it?"

"Does that mean you are feeling better?" I asked carefully.

"If you are asking, Cath, do I think I'm dying? The answer is no. Well, we're all dying, but do I think I'll be leaving you soon? Not if I can help it."

"Thank goodness." I sighed and looked to Bea for a nod of relief but only saw her back. She sniffled, and I knew she was crying with relief. I left her as she chopped veggies and walnuts for her special salads.

"I wanted to go to the bunker. I thought that I was safe inside, but this thing was not interested in sitting and waiting like most cats do. It was going to find a way in."

"What did you do?" Bea asked, finally turning around and wiping the tears from her cheeks.

"Before or after it rammed the door a second time? Well, I ran to the kitchen and grabbed a bag of salt. I sprinkled it around, as you can see." She pointed to the door and the windows.

"Why do you think it didn't smash through the windows? They would have been a lot easier to break, I'd think." Bea asked.

"I'm sure he would have if I hadn't whipped up a binding spell on the spot. Since I didn't know what kind of creature this was, I couldn't constrain *it* and hope those constraints would hold. But I could bind the windows." My aunt swallowed hard. "I could tell by its face it wasn't expecting that. Well, two can play the game of deceit when it's life or death hanging in the balance."

I looked at my watch. It would be another half hour before we cracked the door. The café was already filled with the smell of baking pie, some kind of sweet gingerbread thing, and coffee.

When I turned to check on Treacle, he was sitting on a chair, staring out the window.

"When it tried to crash through the windows, they became pliable. They'd stretch and bend, but they would not break. The thing made sure I didn't get to the back exit. I couldn't leave through the front, obviously. Although I was terrified as it stared at me with those sickly, glowing yellow eyes, I knew I couldn't leave to go to the bunker. I was afraid it might break through my spell. So I stayed here. I dodged its paws, which pushed and scratched and tried to puncture the glass. Hiding behind the counter until the sun came up was my only option. I just prayed the beast would be gone before you girls arrived. And it was."

Bea looked at me, then her mother, and then me again.

"I don't know if this means anything," Bea started. "But last night I woke up and looked out the bedroom window. I thought I saw tracks through the backyard in the little dusting of snow we had. But I thought they were too big. There had to be another explanation. I was groggy and went back to bed. I wonder..."

Aunt Astrid and Bea looked at me.

"Sorry, I slept like a rock," I admitted, biting my lower lip.

"So do you know what this thing is?" Bea pressed.

"When the sun started to come up and the light began to sweep away the shadows, I watched this creature become more agitated." Aunt Astrid leaned forward in her seat. "It knew it was running out of time and it hadn't caught me. It charged the door two more times, the last time injuring itself. I saw the blood. Then I saw it start to shift."

"What?" I didn't understand what she meant.

"It was like that giant, grotesque thing was folding in on itself. With each disgusting part that it turned under, it seemed to melt into the surroundings. It was still there, but it was not in the same form. It was smaller and nearly invisible."

"A giant invisible attacking hairless cat. Nothing we can't handle." I polished my nails on my shirt.

"No. Not invisible." Aunt Astrid wagged her index finger in the air. "Almost invisible. It reflected the light differently, so you might see a ripple or what looks like heat mirages coming off the pavement on a hot day."

"Like in that movie with the thing that blends into the jungle and hunts humans." I pointed to Bea, who shook her head and shrugged. She had no idea what I was talking about.

"It's still out there." Aunt Astrid once again took on her starry gaze as she looked out the window. "So we need to find out as much as we can about it."

"How are we going to do that?" Bea asked. "I've never heard of anything like this, and are you guys not realizing the bigger picture here?"

I looked at my aunt, who shrugged.

"It was obviously after Mom for a reason. Maybe it had something to do with me losing time and Cath getting caught up in that weird vortex that only she and Treacle could see."

"And those giant cat footprints," I added. "My gosh. Do you think it's after us? Do you think it knows who we are?"

"And the missing children," Aunt Astrid replied. "If it is, it has been here studying us for quite some time. I've been sensing it for a while. When I think back, I'm almost positive I saw it but thought my eyes were playing tricks on me. Imagine that, my eyes playing tricks on me. It isn't enough I can see through this dimension to the next and the next. The question really should be when do my eyes *not* play tricks on me?" She smiled mischievously.

"So what do we do?" Bea wiped her hands on her apron and walked to the door to unlock it. We were open for business in just a few more minutes.

"Tonight." My aunt looked like Clint Eastwood as Dirty Harry as she spoke. "My house. We'll find out its name, its purpose, and how we can destroy it."

"Will there be food there?" I had to ask. "Tom is picking me up, and we might go to dinner."

"Tell him to bring you straight to my house after he's fed you," Aunt Astrid teased. "But there will be food at my house. When is there not food at my house?"

"When Bea makes it," I said. "Just remember I'm on a no-tofu diet."

"Hardy-har-har. You're hilarious." Bea rolled her eyes.

Lyle

✣

After our fantastic meal the previous night at the Bibich football game, where the home team lost 7-0, Tom took me to an actual restaurant with linen napkins and real silverware before heading over to my aunt's house.

"I meant to tell you that is an interesting sweater." He smiled as he helped me put on my coat.

"This one is actually my favorite." I stretched it out in front of me, making one little lonely bell on the red nose of Rudolph jingle happily. It had all the reindeer in white silhouette knitted onto a black background, but it was the actual red and green lights attached to the sleigh that blinked that made the sweater so delightfully tacky. "The battery goes in the hem of the sweater. I don't even feel it."

"Only a really beautiful woman could make a sweater like that look sexy."

"Who are you fooling?" I said awkwardly.

"I'm telling the truth," Tom said as he wrapped his arms around me while holding my coat. "In fact, I think you could probably make a potato sack look sexy."

"Thanks." I blushed and looked down at his strong hands. He nuzzled his face into my neck and squeezed me tightly for just a second before letting me go. He took my hand and led me outside to his truck. We got in.

"Did you have enough to eat?" he asked. "I could stop by Mama Tish's for some Italian ice if you'd like. Nothing tastes better on a cold, frosty night than Italian ice."

"No. I'm sure Aunt Astrid has something at her house. You are more than welcome to come in for a spell and say hello," I added.

"I think I'll do that. I'd like to see how she's doing. What an ordeal this morning. Did everyone else believe the bird-flying-into-the-door story?"

I looked at Tom and blinked.

"What are you talking about?" I sounded completely stupid.

"Cath, not so long ago, you and I were in a

haunted part of the woods behind a fallen tree, with a witch trying to sniff us out as if she were a pig and we were truffles. Did you really expect me to believe there wouldn't be a few more weird experiences on the horizon if I hung around you and your family?"

"I just didn't want to assume you were comfortable with all of this." I looked out the window. The houses were all decorated in such beautiful lights they reminded me of gingerbread houses.

"I haven't proven to you I'm comfortable?"

"Well, you might be now, but I have a feeling things are going to get really weird really quickly." I felt a shiver run down my spine as I thought of the thing Aunt Astrid described.

"Well, I certainly do hope so." He winked at me.

Soon, he pulled into my aunt's driveway.

I recognized Blake's sedan and wondered what he was doing there but said nothing out loud. When Tom and I walked into the house, I felt heaviness in the room.

"Hi." I smiled. "Don't tell me you guys ate all the dessert."

"Hey, Cath. Tom, it's nice to see you again," Aunt Astrid said. "I didn't get a chance to tell you thanks for stopping by this morning."

"No worries. How are you feeling?" Tom asked as he went up and planted a kiss on her cheek.

"Right as rain, but we've had a little bad news."

I did a quick head count. Aunt Astrid, Bea, and Jake were all accounted for. Even Blake was there, and of course Tom was safe.

"We found the Lyle boy this afternoon," Jake said.

I held my breath.

"He's dead."

Diabolus Formarum Catus

❦

I slapped my hand over my mouth. Poor Melissa. I know I sound like a broken record, but why did this have to happen just before Christmas?

"Do you have any idea what happened?" I took off my coat and took Tom's to hang up.

"His body looked like it had been partially eaten. We think that Bruce had been out there for a while and some of the coyotes or even the cougars from up north may have stumbled onto him," Jake stated with that monotone that seemed to surface when he was giving especially troubling news. "There was also a storage facility nearby. Store-n-lock. There is a unit rented out to Mr. Gale Wayne."

"I'm not convinced it was him," Blake piped up. "The wounds inflicted on the body do not match any animals that could have gotten to him. The size, width, depth, and even the remains left behind are inconsistent with just about anything that is native to this area."

"So what?" Jake snapped. "It doesn't change the fact that Wayne has a storage unit that he didn't bother to tell any of us about. With all the rumors and accusations, I can't help but think if he really didn't have anything to hide, he would have mentioned that."

"Has anyone spoken to him?" Tom asked, joining the men on the far side of the kitchen at the table. I took a seat next to Bea as Aunt Astrid sliced me a thick slice of chocolate cake.

"Did you make this?" I whispered to Bea, who shook her head no. "Good."

She elbowed me before we continued to listen in on the gruesome details.

"We are in the process of getting a search warrant for the storage unit and his house. It should be ready by tomorrow." Jake nodded. "I'm just hoping we aren't too late to find the girl. In fact, Blake, would you mind taking a run with me back to the storage area? The owner said those surveillance cameras were deleted every three days. I'm wondering if there are any along the route we might be able to tap into."

"The Checked Inn is a pub just a stretch up the road from that storage place," Tom added. "I know the owner, and I'm pretty sure he's got cameras in his parking lot. We can see if they can be of any use. I'll buy you guys a cold one, too."

"That sounds like the best offer I've had all day," Blake mumbled. He turned and smiled at me as if he were looking for some kind of approval. As if he were saying, "See, I can play nice." I couldn't help it. I smiled back.

Once the men left, my aunt pulled out some dusty books I had never seen before. They smelled slightly moldy, and a lot of the script was very hard to read.

"Where did these come from?" Bea asked. "I've never seen them."

"The basement," Aunt Astrid chirped. "I don't like to bring these out very often. They are very old and delicate. Here, wear these." She handed Bea and me each a pair of latex gloves.

"My gosh, could they fall apart that easily?" Bea asked.

"No. The magic is so powerful it may rub off on

your skin. You could end up conjuring a toad-eating demon without even knowing it."

"Oh, I had that happen to me once," I quipped as I snapped on my gloves. "Yes, it produced Darla Castellano. I've yet to figure out how to banish her for good."

Bea laughed, and my aunt rolled her eyes.

"This is serious business," Aunt Astrid assured us as she put on her own latex gloves, then she hoisted a large book up in her hands and led us to her sitting room.

This was a smaller room off the main hallway that was filled with comfy chairs and good lighting and smelled of incense. Bea and I knew this was where she kept many of her precious objects, like her wand, which only came out on special occasions, crystals from various paranormal places around the country, and a crystal ball that she used as a paperweight on her desk. Neither Bea nor I had ever seen her use the crystal ball, but it was there just in case.

The side tables had already been covered with newspaper to catch any magical spillage.

I took a seat on one side of a very worn, tattered love seat that had at one time been covered in a bright-pink-and-green rose pattern but had since faded to what I thought were lovely, dusty tones. Bea sat next to me. Each of us had our own side table and light to work under.

"This is just like studying in high school," she whispered.

"Yeah, except I usually had some magazines or a horror novel to read that was much more interesting than algebra." I snickered.

As we began looking carefully through my aunt's ancient tomes, Aunt Astrid began to quietly recite some kind of incantation. She lit her incense and a couple of candles and then ground a few spices and some salt into her mortar. Once that was done, she walked over to the door and smudged a little of the concoction over the top of the two windows that faced east.

"I've invited some of our ancestors to give us a hand if they can. They'll pass through the door or the windows but leave the riffraff out in the cold," she said, finally letting us in on her plan. "Maybe they'll work quickly."

The words in the book I was looking through reminded me of the writing seen in The Lord of the Rings. It was swirly and curlicued and very elegant but nothing I could make heads or tails of.

But I watched as the words suddenly shifted over the page. It was like watching sea anemones wave with the invisible currents under the water until finally they fell into place, making words I could read.

"That was a neat trick," I mumbled.

"Can you read it all now?" Bea asked. I nodded, and she did too.

Aunt Astrid retrieved her own book, and in the comfortable silence of the house, we searched for a description, a picture, or any mention of the creature Aunt Astrid had been attacked by. It wasn't until almost eleven o'clock that I read and reread a paragraph that sounded so terrifying that I prayed I was wrong and it wasn't the beast we were actually going to have to deal with.

"Aunt Astrid?" I hesitated. "I think I might have found something."

She looked at me and nodded. I felt like a student in school being called to stand up and read a note I had passed out loud in front of everyone.

"It says here that during the yuletide season, the underworld spits forth its young to feed off the precious flesh of innocents. Diabolus Formarum Catus." I gulped. "The great demonic offspring slip through the dimensions unseen. They walk bravely among humans. They choose the most vulnerable and not only eat their bodies, but also drink in the suffering that is a residual effect of their appetites."

"Does it say what they look like?" Bea asked.

"Yeah. It does. It's gross," I said. "It says here that after being spit forth, they writhe in their naked skin, which becomes thicker and fatter the more they consume. The number of wrinkles etched into the flesh indicates how many centuries they've been doing what they are doing."

"Like the rings on a tree," Aunt Astrid said.

"It also says it can maneuver through this plane of existence in this form completely invisible but that it tires easily and its most comfortable configuration is that of a son of Cain."

"Cain?" Bea asked.

"Cain murdered his brother, Abel, in the Bible. Interesting." Aunt Astrid took a deep breath. "That does sound like our guy. Does it say anything about stopping him?"

"It says he was stopped back in oh, some time and dimension that I've never heard of by a dude who…" My mouth instantly went dry. "A dude whose last name was Greenstone."

Bea stared at me with her mouth open. I did the same to Aunt Astrid.

"That thing didn't just happen to mosey up to the

café." I choked. "It didn't just show up as a snow-storm in front of my house, and it didn't randomly leave tracks outside Bea's place. It knows who we are."

"Well, that sounds about right." Aunt Astrid squared her shoulders and clenched her jaw. I had expected some kind of pep talk or inspirational hoo-ha, but I guess my aunt wasn't in the mood. "That's a good start. It tells us what we are dealing with."

"What does it mean that he likes to walk around as a son of Cain?" Bea asked.

"It likes to walk around in human skin," Aunt Astrid almost whispered. "It likes to look like one of us."

She quickly hustled over to a small writing desk that was tucked into the corner of the room. After snapping on a floor lamp to give her more light, she proceeded to look through several newspapers.

"Yes!" she exclaimed. "Here. The first mention of the trouble at Bibich High School." Quickly, she grabbed a calendar and began counting days. "Tech-nically, the yuletide season hadn't begun when this first hit the news." She scratched her head.

"But when did Bruce get reported missing?" I asked.

"That was after it had started." Aunt Astrid

balked. "Maybe I'm just wishing there was a correlation so that I won't have to admit there are two monsters out there. One from another dimension, and one born and raised right here among us."

"Well, Bruce was reported missing ten days ago. But he had been gone two days before that, right? Didn't Melissa wait before calling the police, expecting him to just come home?"

Aunt Astrid snapped her fingers, looked at her calendar, and nodded. I looked at Bea, who smiled.

"I'm still not sure I'm following the connection with Bibich High School," I whispered to Bea. "Do you get it?"

"I have no idea where my mother is going with this, but I bet she'll explain it, won't you, Mom?"

"Try this on for size." Aunt Astrid took a seat. "Mr. Wayne is accused of hurting some children. He denies it. Maybe it's true, maybe it isn't. But two of the children involved go missing. We just found out one of them is dead and was found where Mr. Wayne had a storage unit. Perhaps he is the monster that came to our café."

"But that guy's been at the school for a couple years. Why wait? Why now? If he has a beef with the Greenstone bloodline, what was he waiting for?" I

asked. "If it were me, I'd want my revenge immediately."

"I think what we may need to do is pay a visit to
Mr. Wayne's house." Aunt Astrid sounded as if she
were dreaming up vacation plans to Hawaii.

"We better do that quickly," Bea chimed in. "You
heard Jake. They've requested a search warrant and
expect it to be ready tomorrow morning."

"And we can't step out of this house and over
there without the grandest protection spell ever cast.
That takes time and energy." My aunt tapped her lip
with her index finger before shrugging. "Sorry, girls.
Looks like we'll be pulling an all-nighter tonight."

"Yay! Slumber party!" I clapped. "I call dibs on
the last of the chocolate cake."

Fierce Trio of Felines

❧❧❧

Before I could enjoy my chocolate cake, my aunt, her cat, Marshmallow, my cousin, and I had to traipse across the street to pick up Treacle and then back to Bea's for Peanut Butter in order to safely return to my aunt's house and get the party started.

"I was sleeping," Treacle meowed as he nuzzled my chin.

"You're always sleeping when you stay indoors," I answered.

Once we were all safely behind the locked doors and the protection spell of Aunt Astrid's house, I explained the situation to our three furry companions.

"This is serious business. We need a protection spell like no other. We just found out a thing has a vendetta against us

Greenstones, and well, we want to make sure it knows if we beat it once, we'll do it again. Is that enough of a pep talk for you?"

"Is it the big cat?" Treacle asked, looking at me strangely without his usual purring.

"It is," I answered seriously.

"Which one?"

"What do you mean which one?" My breath hitched in my throat. I looked at Bea and my aunt as they got all of our necessary supplies ready to begin our enchantment.

"There are two big cats." Marshmallow stood at my feet, looking up at me like a statue.

My eyes flitted to Peanut Butter, who I should have known would agree.

The big cat was outside his house, leaving footprints.

I informed my aunt and Bea. They both froze for a moment as they listened.

"It doesn't change anything," Aunt Astrid replied. I heard a slight tremor in her voice. "One cat or a dozen. They are responsible for killing Bruce Lyle and maybe Donna Flint. We have to stop them."

The preparation ceremony went long into the night. The cats took their places at our sides as we Greenstone witches called upon the elements of nature and those things supernatural to give us protection as we sought to get the dimensions in balance once again.

Finally, as the sun came up, we were ready, or at least as ready as we were ever going to be.

"Okay, my fierce trio of felines." I sat down on the floor with the cats. *"You'll need to stay here and keep the home fires burning. We will be going to Mr. Wayne's house and hopefully will find out what he might know about this cat or cats that eat children."* I gave them each a thorough scratch behind the ears.

"Be careful," Treacle ordered.

"I will."

"I should have driven," Bea complained from the backseat.

"Bea, how many times do we have to go over this? You are a terrible driver." I scoffed as I put the pedal to the metal.

It had been alarmingly simple to find out where Mr. Wayne lived. Aunt Astrid was ready to do a location spell that could have easily led us to him, but instead we just looked him up online at the Bibich

High School website. There it was, all over the screen.

"I am not," Bea protested. "I obey all the rules of the road, including the speed limit."

"Riding with you is the real-life version of *Driving Miss Daisy*," I teased. I had to. I was terrified on the inside, and it was my only method of defense. "I just didn't think we had the luxury of letting the snails and turtles beat us to Wayne's house. I thought we wanted to get there before your husband and the po-po arrived."

"Po-po?" Bea giggled.

"Yes. The po-po. The police. Don't you know street talk?"

"No. And neither do you." She laughed outright.

"You two girls need to settle down." Aunt Astrid smiled. "How is it that when it comes to life and death, you two can giggle like the inmates of an insane asylum, but one of you eating kale and the other daring to bite into a hamburger sends you off the rails?"

"Priorities," I answered.

"Okay, speed demon." Bea leaned forward in the backseat. "We should be coming up to it. Slow down. Don't park in the driveway."

"You don't think I should?" I whispered sarcastically. "Aren't we going to just go up and ring the bell?"

"Girls. Center yourselves."

I winked at Bea in the rearview mirror, and she stuck her tongue out at me. I had a flash to the future, where Bea and I would be old and as wrinkled as this cat Aunt Astrid saw, winking and sticking our tongues out at each other. We would be those two giggly girls but not in an insane asylum, just an old folks' home.

As luck would have it, just as I killed the engine, the front porch light of the house at 3443 Pinto Street went off. The front door opened up, and one very angry-looking Mr. Wayne walked out of his house and to his garage.

"He's leaving," Bea muttered as we carefully watched from a few doors down and across the street.

Mr. Wayne was not leaving. Where would he be going? He was suspended from work. As far as anyone knew, he didn't have another job or even family to visit. He strolled out of the house in sweatpants and a T-shirt, seeming to be oblivious to the cold, and walked to the edge of the street to pick up his newspaper.

He looked around quickly as if half expecting

some kind of ambush, but we all ducked down in the car before he saw us.

"Well, we can't very well just go let ourselves in his house." Bea bit her thumbnail. "What should we do?"

"I know exactly what we are going to do." Aunt Astrid looked as if she were having a blast. "Arrhythmias," she whispered as she opened her door, and before Bea or I knew it, she was hustling up the lawn to the front door.

The grass on his lawn was high, and the cold dampness of the frost darkened the cuffs of my jeans and seeped through my Converse All-Stars. Looking around, I was relieved not to see any joggers or dog walkers on the street, coming in our direction.

The Wayne home was a simple ranch-style place with very few bushes and shrubs in the yard to keep up with. It looked as if a single man lived there.

"We shouldn't be standing on the front porch," Bea suggested. Aunt Astrid held her finger to her lips, indicating we should be quiet. The neighborhood was quiet, too. Not a single dog barked, and there wasn't even the echo of the traffic off of Wolf Road to break up the quiet. I did hear one lonely cricket chirping at his buddies who had already retreated in order to sleep for the winter.

Or die, my thoughts interrupted me. *They could have all died. There could be something at this house that silenced the dogs, that killed all the crickets, and who knows what it will do to us.*

No. I was just spooking myself. I had the tendency to do that, and now was no exception. My aunt's sudden burst of energy reminded me of when Treacle was a kitten and had enjoyed a little too much catnip one particular summer afternoon. It was hilarious but not nearly this dangerous.

"Take hands, girls," Aunt Astrid ordered while we stood on Mr. Wayne's front porch, in the early morning, out in the wide open for any neighbor or passerby to see.

Aunt Astrid muttered a few words, and I watched as the breeze bent the trees at the very top and the clouds rolled over themselves. But before I realized what was happening, I witnessed everything slowing down. A few snowflakes drifted down in slow motion as if they were suspended from wires being controlled from somewhere above the clouds.

"What's happening?" Bea asked.

A Delicate Spell

❦

"Time is slowing down," Aunt Astrid explained. "This was a common spell used many years ago when in the spring the boys and girls would get together for the first dance of the season. They'd slow the time down so they could enjoy themselves under canopies of ivy or at the base of old oak trees."

"How come you never told us about this spell?" I asked. "This could have come in handy when I was suffering through high school."

"That's why. Now, this is a very delicate spell. It doesn't last long, and if anyone else shows up, it can come to an abrupt end."

I shrugged and nodded. Of course it wasn't safe and could come to an abrupt end. Who said being a witch spared you from all of life's annoyances.

"We can get into his house, search around, and be out of there before he even has any idea what's happening," my aunt said.

"But what if he sees us? Won't that break the spell?" I asked.

"No. He is under the spell with us. He will only see a few shadows out of the corner of his eye. That's all. It's nothing out of the ordinary that regular people shrug off a hundred times a day."

"This could be fun," Bea whispered.

"Well, it's better than exercising in the morning. I'll say that."

Aunt Astrid grabbed the door handle and gave it a good turn. It opened normally, but as we walked in like a marching band, Mr. Wayne looked as if he was standing stock-still. Except he wasn't. He was in the process of walking to the kitchen, but he was moving at a pace that defied the laws of physics. He moved a fraction of an inch in a minute. I walked right up to him and looked him in the face. He didn't look at me.

"This is weird," I complained as Bea shut the door behind us.

"Let's get to work, ladies. We don't have a lot of time. Oh, ha-ha. Did you hear what I just said?"

Aunt Astrid giggled at her own quip. I hate to admit it, but I giggled, too. Bea rolled her eyes.

I quickly hurried down the only hallway in the small house, and I found his bedroom. It was plain and uninspiring. The bed had not been made, and there were clothes on the floor. Suddenly, I felt guilty about being there. It was one thing for the police to obtain a search warrant and go through a suspect's things. But it was another for us to do it. His under-wear drawer and his laundry were quite personal. As was his medicine cabinet, which held a prescription bottle of sleeping pills.

"If you're going to do this, Cath, just be respect-ful," I tried to comfort myself. But it still didn't make the situation feel any better. Thankfully, I found nothing out of the ordinary in his bedroom or the bathroom. There was an office at the other end of the hallway. As I emerged from my end, I saw Bea standing in front of Mr. Wayne.

"How's it coming?" I asked her quietly just in case he could hear us.

"I'm not getting a reading on him." She shook her head. "I can't touch him, or else I risk breaking our time-altering spell. But I get a sense that he is hiding something."

"Would it help to handle some of his *personals*?" I whispered.

Bea looked at me, and I thought for a moment she was going to call me some kind of pervert and recoil in disgust.

"That's worth a try. Good call."

I led my cousin to the bedroom, and she picked up a shirt that had been lying on the floor. There was nothing special about it, nothing like blood spatter or telltale tears. But I could tell by Bea's reaction she had found something.

"He's feeling guilty about something," she said. As she looked down at the shirt and twisted it in her hands, I could see she was trying to dig deeper. "But it could be anything. I can't see anything that would tell me for sure if he had anything to do with Bruce's death or if he felt guilty he forgot to pay his electric bill on time. It's all muddled up. Residual." She looked at me helplessly. "I need to touch his skin if I'm going to find out any more."

We started to walk back to the kitchen but heard something slam.

"What was that?" I grabbed Bea's arm.

"Mom." Her eyes widened. We both dashed down the hallway past Mr. Wayne, who was still in the same position we had left him in with the exception that his right foot was a little higher in the back than it had been ten minutes ago. As we rounded the corner into the family room, we saw Aunt Astrid standing in front of a door she was holding shut. She was sweating.

"Did you find something?" I asked stupidly.

"Did I." She swallowed hard. "There's a portal in there." She jerked her head toward the door.

"What?" I gasped.

Carefully, Aunt Astrid took the doorknob in both hands and turned it slowly. She gently eased the door open.

"Yikes!" I clutched Bea's arm. "He has paneling on the walls! The horror!"

My aunt turned then looked at us both. We didn't see anything, but it was obvious she did.

"It's right there, and it's big," she said.

"So what does it mean?" I asked.

"It means that Mr. Wayne has some special abilities, and I think he's had more than a hand in the disappearances of those children."

"I wanted to get a reading from him, but I was afraid to touch him for fear of shattering our spell. Which is working quite nicely, I have to admit," Bea said. "I could only tell from his clothes that he's feeling guilty about something, but I don't know what. It could be anything."

"Maybe we could tie him up really fast, then he won't know what hit him when the spell is broken, and you can get a reading on him that way," I suggested. "We could slip a pillowcase over his head and trip him, and Aunt Astrid and I could sit on him until you get a reading."

"Sit on him?" My aunt looked at me as if I'd suggested she shave her head.

"I don't know," I whined. "I'm just trying to help."

"We are running out of options, and Mom, didn't you say this spell didn't last very long? We are probably already on borrowed time, standing here trying to come up with something. Personally, I like Cath's idea. The element of surprise is in our favor."

"Right?" I smiled. "I'll get a pillowcase." I dashed off toward the bedroom and yanked the pillow from the bed. Pulling it from the case as I ran back, I thought I saw something moving past the window.

When I came back into the front room, Bea and Aunt Astrid were not there. My heart rate started to quicken. It was funny because so did Mr. Wayne. Before he could become completely reanimated, I heard Bea whistle and dashed toward the spare room where the portal was.

"There are men on the porch," she whispered.

"What?" I went to peek out the window, but Aunt Astrid grabbed my arm.

"It's Jake and Blake with their search warrants. As soon as they pound on that door, the spell will be broken, and they are going to find three trespassers who they happen to know hiding in this room."

"Oh man!" I bit my lip. "I've seen movies where the police conduct a search with a warrant. There is nowhere to hide. We are cooked. Do you think we can run out the back door?"

"I'm sure Jake would have that covered in case Wayne decided to try and flee," Bea added.

"We have no choice." Aunt Astrid took both our hands. "We have to enter the portal."

"I'd rather take my chances with Jake," I argued. "A portal? Can't that lead to anywhere? Couldn't we end up in an alternate universe where, I don't know, spiders are kept as pets and people are required to eat brown rice all the time?" I was nearly crying I was so scared.

"Mom, if we go in there, we might not come out. That's a chance, isn't it?"

"And what do you think will happen if your

husband finds us? He'll lose his job. You and me and Cath will all be in jail. There are no magic spells that would get us off the hook. Either we stay and take our chances that the law will take pity on us, or we hide in this portal until the coast is clear."

Bea and I looked at each other. I searched the room, hoping for a closet or a trapdoor that hid a tunnel that led outside, but there was nothing. We heard Jake's voice outside the door as he demanded Mr. Wayne open up and said that they had a search warrant. There was a lot of shuffling around, and the noise that came from behind that door was terrifying.

"Planecia Penes," Aunt Astrid whispered harshly.

Quickly, I took my cousin's hand, and before either one of us could protest, we watched Aunt Astrid step into nothingness. We followed her carefully.

Psychedelic Roller Coaster

❧❦❧

As far as portals go, this was not at all what I expected. I've seen artwork of glowing green or blue mirror-like images floating behind decorative frames that are the entry and exit point of the portals. They look mystical and pretty and luminous as the possibility of entering other worlds flickers there.

There was a television show that showed people slipping and sliding through dimensions like they were on a psychedelic roller coaster, and The Doctor travels in his phone booth through clouds and lightning and all kinds of crazy stuff. I think my favorite was Captain Kirk and Spock jumping into a giant ring, their forms freezing in mid-jump only to come tumbling out the other side.

So that is what I had to compare this with. I was

terrified, but what happened was almost laughable.

"This is it?" I grumbled.

"Looks that way," Aunt Astrid said as she held tightly to the edge of the rocky cave we were standing in.

"How come we aren't tumbling through space and time or being blinded by flashes of pink and blue lights?"

"You say that like that's what you were hoping would happen," Bea said. "I'm just fine with loitering around right here until we can slip back out. We can slip back out again, right, Mom?"

I turned around and looked behind us. The tunnel ran on and on into a very black hole. Part of me wanted to venture back there, but as I leaned a little closer, I thought I could hear something.

"As long as we stay grounded right here, we should be able to walk right back out. The portal is meant for things to enter that specific place. Mr. Wayne's home. He put it there," Aunt Astrid said as she pushed her curling gray-and-red locks from her face. "I can only assume he did it so he could come and go as he wanted."

"Where do you think he went?" I asked. "I mean, do you have any idea where this portal might lead?"

My aunt shook her head.

"How about you, Bea?" I was really talking to keep my nerve, not because I really wanted to know anything. The problem was that I thought I was hearing something behind us but it was so dark.

"I'm not sure what I'm feeling, to be quite honest." Bea licked her lips. "I didn't get a reading on Mr. Wayne, my husband is just a few feet from me in another dimension, and I'm in a creepy cave that looks like dirt and rock but yet not like dirt from our planet. No. I'm pretty much useless right now."

I was still holding her hand and gave it a squeeze.

"It's all right, Bea. Right, Aunt Astrid? We're together, and we aren't moving from this spot." I tried to sound confident. "We can see the light of our world right there, and it gives us enough light to see each other. We're doing pretty good. Yeah, I'd say pretty good."

It started like a few pebbles falling along the side of the wall.

I didn't look behind me. I didn't say anything to Bea or my aunt. I just kept talking. I couldn't say what I was talking about. It was all jumbled together, and I don't even think the words were making any sense. But finally I couldn't resist any more.

"Do you hear that?" I whispered, cutting myself off in midsentence.

Both Bea and my aunt nodded. It was as if they had heard them all along but were just trying to humor me.

Yes. At first it sounded like pebbles sliding down a wall. But then it sounded more as though something was walking behind us. Something that could maneuver in that pitch darkness and wasn't afraid of it. It was getting louder as it was getting closer.

"None of us has any kind of light, do we?" I asked hopefully, but they both shook their heads no. I swallowed hard, and still holding Bea's hand, I stepped a little farther back into the tunnel.

"Cath," she said. "No."

"Maybe it's nothing bad," I said, but the quiver in my voice totally betrayed me.

The scraping stopped. I held my breath and listened. Just as my shoulders started to relax and my breath came back, I heard the shuffling again. This time it was fast. As if whatever it was was pushing itself through the tight tunnel, hurrying to catch the intruders that had stumbled into its lair.

Without thinking, I backed up and held close to Bea. My aunt, who was still staring at the portal entrance—or exit, depending on if you saw the cup as half-empty or half-full—was not paying any attention to the thing coming up behind us.

"We're almost there, girls," she assured us.

"How can you be sure?" Bea whispered, her fingers digging into my hand.

"I can see the men leaving. At least, I think they are."

"Aunt Astrid, something is coming." I balked. "I think it's big."

"Don't look behind us, girls," Aunt Astrid instructed.

Bea turned her back to the darkness, but I couldn't help myself. I looked back. I heard the shuffling get faster, and then, like a shard of ice through my heart, I heard that horrible sound Aunt Astrid described that she heard at the café.

"Aunt Astrid, I think it's close," I whispered. My mouth had gone bone-dry, and all the hairs were up on my neck. I tried to think of something to calm myself down, but it wasn't working. All I heard were the shuffling steps and the guttural, hateful meow.

Cats killed for sport. Killer whales did, too. But I was pretty confident there wasn't a killer whale behind us. Cats not only killed for sport, but they also liked to torture their prey. They'd box them in then let them get away for a moment, only to pounce again.

You can bet that I suddenly felt an uncomfortable

kinship with the lab rats that were made to run mazes.

"Don't look behind us, girls," Aunt Astrid said soothingly. I could feel the sweat in her palms as she took hold of my hand and Bea's. "Just don't look."

My body began to tremble. I looked at Bea, who did exactly what her mother instructed. I, on the other hand, was my mother's daughter. My mother was the reckless one. The one who would risk everything, even her own life, for her daughter. She gave up everything to save me. She was pulled into a portal, too. But Aunt Astrid said she had died when that happened.

Maybe she did.

Don't be ridiculous, Cath. My thoughts were like jigsaw puzzle pieces struggling to fit together to give me a complete picture instead of fragments. *Your mother is not down this portal. She couldn't be. That was almost twenty years ago. No. What's back there is bad. What's back there isn't the pretty, kind, and spontaneous thing that was Mama. It's a monster.*

"Don't look back, girls," Aunt Astrid repeated. "And get ready to jump when I say so. One. Don't look back. Two." I felt Bea squeeze my hand tightly. "Don't look back. Three! Jump!"

Before I jumped, before Aunt Astrid said three, I

looked back. I saw the orange eyes and the skin wrinkled like the texture of the human brain. I saw it, and it saw me. That creature saw me. Maybe I was just imagining things or the darkness was playing tricks on me. That can happen. Terror can make a person see and hear and even smell things that weren't there. But I swear that beast grinned. It looked as if it recognized me and grinned.

Suddenly, I was toppling on top of Bea and Aunt Astrid on the carpeted floor of the paneled office of Mr. Wayne.

"Dear Lord!" Bea gasped. "How long were we in there?"

"I hope it wasn't that long, or else it might mean we missed opening up the café. That's not good for this time of year," my aunt said. I could see she was just trying to bring a little normalcy back into us since we were all obviously scared out of our wits. She trembled when I reached for her hand to help her up, and her hair was matted to her forehead.

Bea still looked as if she could do a fashion shoot, but she had tears in her eyes.

"Let's n-not d-do that again," she said. "Can we go back to the café? Can we open up even if it's late? I'd really like to be around some people and hear talk about Christmas and shopping and the weather.

Anything that doesn't include portals and time-bending spells and all that jazz."

"Of course we can, honey." Aunt Astrid took both our hands, and we carefully stepped out of the office. The house had been literally torn apart. Police tape marked off everything. We stepped into the family room and pulled open the front door.

The cold air felt deliciously good, and I inhaled deeply, feeling my lungs tingle.

"The coast is clear," Aunt Astrid said. Quickly, we hurried toward my car, piled in, and headed toward the café. No one spoke until I finally cracked the silence.

"I saw it, Aunt Astrid." My eyes began to fill with tears. It wasn't because I was scared but because it wasn't what I had hoped to see.

Deep down inside, I had hoped that maybe, just maybe, there was a miracle in store for me, and my mother would appear at the end of that dark portal. She'd be just as beautiful as I remembered her, maybe a little rough around the edges, but it would be her. And she'd recognize me. She'd recognize me.

"What did you see, Cath?"

"A cat. A big one."

Tumble

❧

"I t's very weird." Aunt Astrid said as she flipped on all the lights in the café.

I clutched my throat. "What's weird? I can't think of anything that happened at this early hour that could be called weird. Unless you are referring to the fact we hung out in a portal with a giant, ugly, hairless cat creeping up behind us. Nothing else comes to mind."

"That portal was not friendly." Bea made a face as if she'd just swallowed a spoonful of castor oil.

"Did you get the feeling it wasn't Mr. Wayne's portal?" Aunt Astrid asked.

"I did." Bea nodded. "I'm pretty sure he knew it was there but he didn't conjure it. Someone else did. My money is on the other cat."

"Hey, that's my line." I balked. "So do you think

Mr. Wayne is covering for that cat? Keeping it safe or something?"

"I don't know." Aunt Astrid pulled her long hair up and tied it back in a loose ponytail with a rubber band. "But if there are two giant cats, it would not be surprising if they knew each other. It would be pretty hard to maneuver through the streets and not catch sight or scent of each other."

The Brew-Ha-Ha Café wasn't open for business for ten minutes before the place was packed with early-rising Christmas shoppers and visitors, and I couldn't have been happier.

I didn't know what to think about the whole two-cat-portal thing, and I couldn't shake the ridiculous disappointment I had felt seeing that hideous creature instead of my own sweet mom coming up behind us before we jumped back into this dimension.

I was so confused that when Darla Castellano showed up with her latest boyfriend, an older man with a Rolex watch and leather trench coat, I smiled and wished her a Merry Christmas. The words "come see us again soon" even spilled out of my mouth. She had to think I was drunk. I wished I were.

Aunt Astrid did a few holiday fortunes at her

special table in the back of the café for some of her regular visitors. Bea busied herself filling coffee cups and making special teas. I boxed up croissants and brownies and dozens of those gingerbread men that Kevin had immediately baked when he arrived a short while ago. Business was booming, and the Christmas spirit had infiltrated the café, finally chasing the dread of the morning's encounter.

"We should change the name of this place to the Brew-Ho-Ho for Christmastime next year," I suggested to Bea. "Wouldn't that be cute?"

"That is hilarious," she squealed as she added her finishing touches to a couple of her special peppermint and jasmine teas. "I love that idea. We could put it on our bags."

"We could get sweaters with that made on them." I clapped.

"Let's not go crazy." Bea smiled. She looked up and stared out the window for a second. I followed her eyes and saw a familiar face looking in at us. "Do you know that man?" she asked me.

"Um. I've seen him before." I hesitated. "But I don't know him."

"Well, he looks like he knows you." She bumped me with her hip.

It was the guy from the football game. He wore a

long black wool coat and a gray knit cap and had a Band-Aid on his forehead sticking out from beneath it. Before I could say anything else to Bea, the guy started waving me outside.

"Why doesn't he come in?" I asked.

"Perhaps he's shy. It is pretty crowded in here. Go ahead." Bea went back to pouring her teas.

"Are you sure?"

"Yeah. You're not going off to get married, right? You're just going to see what he wants."

I looked at the window again, and then my eyes fell to Darla, who was watching the fellow outside and my reaction as if she were watching a tennis game.

Yes, it was because of her I went outside to see what this handsome stranger wanted. He was even better looking up close, and he smelled like a camp-fire. I folded my arms around me to keep out the cold as best I could and walked up to him.

"I thought I'd never see you again," he said right away.

"Do I know you?" I asked awkwardly. A guy this good-looking had to have me confused with someone else. He wasn't like Tom, who had a rugged, manly uniqueness to him that was made all the more attractive by his sense of humor and, well, his willingness to accept my pointed hat and broom-stick. But this guy looked as if he'd stepped out of a magazine. He had to be at least a foot taller than me, and his shoulders looked as though they could support six acrobats without him even breaking a sweat.

"Not yet." He smiled. "Clyde Tumble." He reached out a black-leather-covered hand. "I saw you at the football game the other night.

"Oh, yes." I nodded politely. "Cath Greenstone." I shook his hand then rubbed my arms to chase away the chill. Strange that I wasn't feeling all that chilly as I looked at Clyde.

"It is wonderful to meet you, Cath Greenstone." He smiled as if he knew what I looked like in my underwear. "I'm wondering when I can take you out for dinner."

"What?" I yapped, giggling nervously. "I have a boyfriend. I'm sorry."

"Well, how about a cup of coffee?" He took a step closer and looked down at me with a very alluring grin. "He wouldn't mind if you had coffee, would he?"

"Probably not, but I work at a coffee shop." I jerked my thumb toward the window. "I can get all the coffee I want. For free. Would you like a cup?"

He looked at his watch and clicked his tongue.

"I'd really like to, but I'm running late." He looked back at me and blinked innocently. "You work here every day?"

I nodded.

"Well, I think I'll be stopping by for coffee when I have a little more time. Save me a seat, would you?" He nodded. "It was very nice to meet you, Cath." His eyes roamed up and down my body before locking with my eyes. "I'll be seeing you."

He looked up at the Brew-Ha-Ha sign then back at me before walking away. Yes, he did do one of those turn around and see if I'm looking looks, and I hated the fact that heat spread from my cheeks and over my forehead, chin, and neck. To add insult to injury, I had to walk in and face my aunt and Bea as they watched me walk in.

"So." Bea leaned over the counter. "Who was that?"

"I'm sorry, but we just came tumbling out of a vortex. Don't you think we have more important things to worry about than my love life?"

"Love life?" Aunt Astrid mused loudly.

"You categorize him as a part of your love life?" Bea tapped her lips, smiling.

"Look, I'm not interested in this dude. I don't

even know him." I shook my head. "I can't even figure out what to get Tom for Christmas. The last thing I need is to involve another guy in the mix."

"You still haven't bought something for Tom?" Bea gasped as if I'd just said I drove my car into her living room window.

"I will." I rolled my eyes. "I'm not Scrooge."

Dead

✥

The cats were lounging around on the various chairs in Aunt Astrid's house when we finally closed the café for the evening.

"Hey, guys." I stepped inside the warm house behind my aunt and cousin. *"Anything exciting happen while we were out?"*

"Where should we start?" Marshmallow asked.

"What happened?" I asked out loud so my family would know our cats had something to report.

"Well, Peanut Butter took a running leap off the banister, and although he landed on his feet, he knocked over those Christmas ornaments." Marshmallow yawned and gave her paw a lick.

My shoulders slumped, and I tilted my head to the left.

"Are you kidding?" I folded my arms and shook my head. *"That's all?"*

"We all felt the ripples from the spell, and from this end, it held. Once everything settled down, we assumed it had worked out," she replied.

"I'm glad no one was worried," I said. *"I'd hate to think any of you guys were worrying about us."* I turned to Bea. "You've got a few broken ornaments." I pointed to the banister, where there were two shattered glass ornaments.

"Do I need to ask which one did this?" Bea walked up to Peanut Butter and scooped the young cat into her arms. The cat nuzzled her underneath her chin and purred loudly.

"I had to get from the banister to the living room immediately. I couldn't waste a single second," he said.

"Okay, girls. I'm afraid that if I smell another gingerbread cookie, I'm going to pass out. How about I defrost some spaghetti and meatballs?" Aunt Astrid said.

"I'm in," I said, scratching Peanut Butter under the chin as I walked up to Treacle, who was stretching his back up, looking like every Halloween decoration that featured a cat. He sat down and looked at me stoically.

"*Hello, handsome.*" I looked at him as he blinked slowly.

"*Hi.*" He sniffed my hand. "*Were you around another cat?*"

"*I'll tell you all about it, but not now. I'm too hungry to think straight.*" I scratched my cat behind his ears and started to walk over to help Aunt Astrid with dinner, when the doorbell rang.

"Be careful," I warned Bea as she went to answer it. "We've had some strange visitors over the past few hours."

"Hi, Tom," I heard her say, and suddenly, my heart was in my throat.

Should I tell him about Clyde Tumble or just keep it to myself? Would he tell me if any woman asked him to coffee? Was it worth mentioning? No. Nope. It wasn't at all. I smiled but knew it was awkward, as if I was hiding something. I don't think I could have acted like a bigger spaz.

"Hi, Tom." Aunt Astrid waved without turning away from the stove. "We're having spaghetti and meatballs. Join us, won't you?"

"I'd love to, Aunt Astrid. Thanks."

He smiled when he came up to me, but he looked as though he'd just run five miles in his cowboy boots without being prepared to run at all.

"What's wrong?" I asked, hoping he wouldn't say he saw me standing outside the café with Clyde Tumble.

"Gale Wayne is dead."

"What?" I hollered. Both my aunt and cousin froze as well.

"Jake and Blake went to his house with a search warrant, and they had another unit pay a visit to his storage facility. They found Donna Flint's body there. It was in the same condition as the Lyle boy's. Just torn apart."

"My gosh." Aunt Astrid shook her head. "Did he try to resist?"

"According to what I heard, and I know Jake and Blake would follow procedure to the letter, he was taken to the station without incident. The guys were in the middle of asking him questions when the other officers radioed in what they found at the storage unit. They said she had been killed in one location and moved there. Maybe Wayne's thinking was to keep it until all this drama with the school died down. Maybe he had something in mind for the remains. We don't know. All we do know is that throughout everything, he said he didn't do it."

"Well, he was accused of two things," Bea interrupted. "Was he talking about the accusations at the school or the kidnapping and murders?"

"Both," Tom said. "He insisted he didn't do anything to any kids in Wonder Falls and that he loved his students and would never hurt them."

"Will Jake be coming home?" Bea's face was serious.

"That's why I'm here." Tom smiled wryly. "Blake called me and asked if I was coming by. I said I'd pass along the information to you and let you know they were going to be tied up for several more hours. The investigation was enough, but now, with the suicide, it's a mess."

"How did he do it?" Aunt Astrid asked before I could. I hate to admit it, but that was exactly what I was thinking. Sure, it's gory and macabre, but I can't help it. I want to know the details.

"Blake said he must have smuggled in some kind of weapon." Tom clenched his fists nervously. "His wrists were sliced open all the way down to the bone. He bled out within a matter of minutes. You'd have to have nerves of steel to do that. But I can't help but think…" I watched him swallow hard as he shook his head. "He might have thought he was going to use that weapon on one of the officers and it just didn't work out that way."

"Oh gosh." Bea gasped, taking hold of her mother's hand.

"I'm sorry." Tom looked at me. "I didn't mean to get so gruesome about it. I just think it's best to get it all out."

"I'm going to call Jake," Bea almost whispered.

"Yes, dear," Aunt Astrid said soothingly. "You go on and use the phone in the study."

Peanut Butter trotted after his mistress as Treacle rubbed back and forth on Tom's leg, and Marshmallow remained on her cushion, calmly listening.

Aunt Astrid continued to prepare dinner. It was just a few minutes, and the smell of oregano and tomato and garlic began to fill the air, making the room feel a good bit cozier.

"Is Bea okay?" Tom asked nervously.

"She worries about Jake." I had to be honest, at least when it came to my family. "Any woman married to a police officer worries that way."

"Would you worry about me that way if we were married?"

"Well, I don't really know you all that well yet." I blinked. "But truthfully, I worry about you running with scissors, using a can opener, chopping onions. Whereas I'm confident in your policing, I'm not so sure about your management of everyday activities."

"Is that so?" He chuckled.

"Yup."

Finally, Bea came back into the kitchen.

"What did Jake have to say?" Aunt Astrid rubbed her daughter's arm as Bea brought down plates from the cabinet.

"Well, he had quite a few things to say."

Tom and I leaned against the counter to listen.

"First, he said that Mr. Wayne did not act like a man who was guilty of the crimes he was being asked about but that he was definitely hiding something. He also said that Blake patted him down before they put him in the squad car at his home."

"If Blake did it, then Mr. Wayne had to have been hiding that weapon in a very intimate place," I said, looking at Tom, who cringed as well.

"That's another thing. There was no weapon found in the cell."

"What?" Tom snapped.

"You were right. Jake confirmed that his wrists were slashed, elbow to wrist, almost to the bone, but they've not found any weapon."

"Ugh." Tom rubbed his stomach. "So what do they think he used?"

"His own fingers and quite possibly his teeth," Bea said. "It's not impossible."

"But it is improbable," Tom insisted. "Unless someone in the station gave him a weapon. I've heard of officers urging inmates to end it all because prison time for a child murderer is the hardest time to do. Could someone there have done that?"

"They've got cameras all over the station, don't they?" I walked around to the pot my aunt had put on the stove and began stirring the pasta, which was bubbling nicely.

"Yeah," Bea agreed. "I'm sure they'll be reviewing them. Internal Affairs will be all over this. Mr. Wayne claimed to have no next of kin, but I guarantee that if there is any kind of lawsuit against the police department, you watch the long-lost relatives start crawling out of the woodwork if they smell a big settlement could be coming."

"Did they mention what else they found at the storage unit?" I asked. "Anything useful there?"

"Aside from the Flint girl's body, there were a couple of bikes, boxes of old tax forms, dishes, tools, and some metal folding chairs."

"That's weird." I took the pot of pasta over to the strainer that was in the sink and dumped the steaming ribbons into it, releasing a mushroom cloud of steam. "So he really did store normal things in his storage unit? There were no Baggies of miscellaneous earrings or bracelets from other victims? No clippings of hair or teeth in Baggies arranged by date? No box o' panties or worn nylons?"

"Where do you get this stuff?" Bea asked, not wanting to chuckle but unable to keep the smile off her face.

"You know weirdos like Mr. Wayne keep trophies. Right?" I nudged Tom for backup. "They all do so they can go back and fondle them and relive the experience. Like normal people hang their diplomas on the wall or report cards on the fridge so they can look at them and be proud, serial killers keep their own twisted version of a certificate indicating a job well done."

"It's sad but true," Tom concurred. "Good one, honey." He patted my back gently and then rubbed it affectionately, making me melt in his direction while I placed a big bowl of spaghetti in front of him.

"I'm suddenly not so hungry," Bea said.

"I'll eat hers." I elbowed Aunt Astrid, who nodded while patting her daughter on the shoulder. "For some reason, this doesn't affect my appetite."

"Well, one thing is for sure," Aunt Astrid said, fixing her own plate and taking a seat at the counter with Tom and me. "Time will tell if Mr. Wayne was the culprit."

"What do you mean?" Tom asked, wiping his mouth with a paper napkin. "He may not have confessed, but finding poor Donna Flint in his storage unit is pretty damning evidence."

"It is," my aunt replied before rolling a huge ball of spaghetti on her fork and shoveling it in her mouth. "But something tells me this isn't over yet."

Santa's Village

❧❦❧

"Y" ou are going to look fantastic," I told Treacle as I put a small headband with reindeer antlers on it on his head.

"*This is so embarrassing.*" He meowed.

"*It isn't. It's fun. Get in the holiday spirit.*" I scratched underneath his chin. "*You will probably be the most handsome pet there. After I put on your bowtie.*"

"*A bowtie?*"

"*Yes. Look.*" I held up the deep-maroon collar with a lovely velvet bowtie attached. "*It's beautiful. It's not tacky or loud. It's a very respectable tie, and I have one to match.*" I held mine up for effect.

"*Are you wearing antlers too?*"

"*Well, I wasn't planning on it, but now that you mention it, that might not be a bad idea.*" I shrugged.

"Bea, Treacle thinks I should wear the antlers, too. What do you think?"

"Well, I'm not sure since Peanut Butter and I will be winning the contest. I don't know if it will make a difference what you do." She smirked.

"Did you hear that?"

"Well, it looks like it is on." Treacle pushed his head against mine as I looked him in the eye.

Treacle came with me to the Brew-Ha-Ha. It was hard for him to adjust to staying inside when the weather got colder. It wasn't a horrible day. The sun was shining, but the wind had kicked up, and that sent the temperature to the low thirties, just a whisker below freezing. I'd promised Treacle he could go out on his own before quitting time and I'd meet him at the house so he could get a little fresh air and run today's cabin fever out of himself.

But for now he was content to let me dress him up as he lounged on the window ledge, looking out onto the bustling sidewalk.

"Bea, your mom is here," I announced, waving to my aunt through the window. She looked as if she had to use the bathroom badly.

"You aren't going to believe this." She huffed as she burst through the front door, setting off the chimes attached to the hinges. "I stay away from the newspapers. You girls know that. But have you seen the *Wonder Falls Bugle*?"

Of course I hadn't. To be honest, I didn't care to read about the new statue in front of the library or how the women's auxiliary was having their annual Winter Dip for the Polar Bears of Wonder Falls to take a swim in the frozen, man-made lake a couple miles out from downtown, or the editorials complaining about parking at the post office.

"We usually don't get it at the house until after noon," Bea said.

"You have a subscription to the *Wonder Falls Bugle*?" I teased.

"I like to support the locals." Bea pouted. "I'll bet you didn't know there was a new sculpture in front of the library. It's of Timothy Monroe."

"Who in the world is Timothy Monroe?" I griped.

"I don't know, but it's a beautiful sculpture. Very lifelike, and you know how much I love bronze statues."

"Would you two quit your babbling and listen?" Aunt Astrid pulled the crumpled newspaper from her beautiful satchel made of a red Indian tapestry. "Look at this."

She spread out the newspaper on the counter. In smaller print than the headline that read Mayor

Announcing New Charter School Qualifications was the line Murder Suspect Commits Suicide During Police Questioning.

"That isn't exactly the most honest headline," Bea whined. "Do they mention they found a body in his storage unit and that maybe this was an admission of guilt?"

"They do, but it's down at the bottom of the article." Aunt Astrid pursed her lips. "But this isn't the end of the story."

"What do you mean?" I scratched Treacle behind the ears.

"While I was at the bank, picking up our deposit bag, I was talking to Lynette Rosette. You know Lynette? She always wears all those gold necklaces and bangle bracelets?"

Bea and I nodded.

"Lynette is very nice." Bea smiled. "She's always got the most pleasant disposition. Her aura sometimes glows pink."

"Oh yeah, the one with the pink aura," I joked. "I know her."

"Well, Lynette told me that another teenager has gone missing."

"You mean Mr. Wayne had killed a third we didn't know about?" I was shocked.

"No." Aunt Astrid took a seat at the counter. "The child disappeared yesterday."

None of us said anything as we let the news sink in.

"Mom. Could it be that this teenager is just a runaway?" Bea asked. "I hate to think that that is a better alternative, but isn't it?"

"His name is Colin. He's a straight-A student," my aunt said. "He was class president. Played in the band. Well liked by just about everyone."

"Did he go to Bibich High School?" I asked.

My aunt nodded sadly.

"So Mr. Wayne was innocent and the killer is still out there?" Bea gasped.

"I wouldn't say he was innocent." My aunt surprised us both. "But it does appear that there is a copycat out there."

I chuckled.

"What's funny?" Bea looked at me.

"A copycat," I said. "It's just kind of funny that we've got a giant cat roaming the streets, invisible, or at least in disguise, and the word associated now with this new development is copycat."

"Yes. It is a bit ironic," my aunt agreed. "But either way, we've got an issue on our hands. Not to mention what Jake and Blake and even Tom are going to do about this. There will certainly be questions, and even at this beautiful time of year, there are some people who never want to let a crisis go to waste. This will get worse before it gets better. I can feel it on several different levels."

"Maybe we shouldn't go to the reindeer contest," I volunteered. "Maybe we should just hang around and…"

"And do what?" my aunt interrupted. "We can't really do anything until we close the café."

"Cath, were you just looking for an excuse to not get beat by Peanut Butter and me?" Bea looked up at the ceiling, as innocent as a slice of peach pie.

"You hear that, Treacle?" I scratched him under the chin but stared at my cousin. "Before we beat the big bad guy in town, we are just going to have to put a little hurtin' on the family."

※

"It's a beautiful day to show you who makes the better reindeer, cuz," Bea taunted as we both left the café, leaving Aunt Astrid and Kevin to handle the lunchtime patrons. "Peanut Butter and I will see you there."

"Yeah, okay," I answered. "We'll keep an eye out for you in the losers' circle."

I was holding Treacle in my arms, where he snuggled contentedly.

"You're really all about the winning, aren't you?" he purred.

"Not really. I just wanted to show you off to the world, that's all."

It was true. As we made our way to the center of town, about four blocks from the café, people pointed and smiled at my beautiful black cat wearing his distinguished bowtie and lightweight antlers, and he'd even allowed me to add a simple Santa hat that matched mine.

Downtown was a winter wonderland. Christmas music was piped through speakers all along the main drag. The lampposts were all adorned with red-and-green banners. Poinsettias were outside almost every storefront. But my favorite was the lights. Even on a gray day like today with the smell of snow in the air, the Christmas lights shined bright.

The majority of the shops had simple white lights, looking very traditional and timelessly classy. But then there were the rogue shops like Something Sweet Candy Shop and Brillows Second Hand bookstore that used what looked like dozens of strands of multicolored bulbs, giving their windows the appearance of being encased in bright, glowing candy. I loved it.

Small sheds representing a dozen different countries popped up in the main square like a Santa's Village. A person could get some decadent homemade fudge, hot chocolates, or even a hot toddy. There was bratwurst and jerk chicken, slices of pizza and egg rolls, and one little shack serving fresh sushi. Everyone working was wearing Santa hats or red-and-green aprons. The air smelled warm and delicious no matter where you walked, and with Christmas just a little over a week away, school was out for the holiday, and there were lots of kids tagging along with their parents.

"I don't think I'd be able to let my child go out and enjoy all this without holding my hand. Not with all the trouble and disappearances going on." I squeezed Treacle. *"It's hard enough letting you go out."*

"I know how to defend myself." He stretched his razor-sharp claws on my arm. *"Kids are, well, stupid."*

I nodded, knowing what he meant. As I looked around, I saw one teenage girl with her coat hanging wide open exposing a very daring T-shirt beneath. A teenage boy was walking with his hands thrust deep in his jean pockets, his shoulders pulled all the way up to his ears, wearing nothing more than a hoodie, and he didn't even have the hood up.

"If they can't figure out how to dress when it's cold, they shouldn't be allowed to go anywhere by themselves. Especially when there might still be a predator out there," I said to Treacle.

But my thoughts weren't going to make a difference. Plus, I'd only heard about the wrath of teenagers when they didn't get their way. I'd never experienced it firsthand. I have the feeling it's probably as nasty as that hairless cat in the portal at the late Mr. Wayne's house, if not worse.

"This way to the reindeer contest," I read on a cute red, white, and green pole with an arrow pointing to a large tent. The sounds of barking dogs could be heard coming from the inside along with a couple of bird squawks and one lonely meow.

"You ready for this?"

"Ready as I'll ever be."

Rock Star

✦✦✦

Once we stepped inside the tent, we felt warm all over. The heat was on high so the pets wouldn't be too chilly. Water bowls were placed randomly around the edges. A small patch of green grass was also situated far from the contestants and the judges for any four-legged friends who might not be able to make it outside for a nature call.

When I saw Bea walk in, she was carrying Peanut Butter in his carrier, which she had decked out like a sleigh.

"Oh brother," I chided as I waved her over. "You sneaky little crafter, you."

"I couldn't help myself." She giggled. "I was struck by the ghost of impossible Christmas projects.

I started on this back in September and still wasn't sure if I was going to finish it on time."

"I got to give it to you, Bea. Peanut Butter's sleigh looks great. Doesn't it, Treacle?

"Are you hating this as much as me?" I heard Peanut Butter ask Treacle.

"Just relax. It won't last too much longer," Treacle replied before yawning.

He was right.

As Bea and I sat next to each other, smiling and admiring all the adorable "reindeer" that had turned out, before we knew it, the judges had made their decision and were awarding a white third-place ribbon, a red second-place ribbon, and final first-place blue ribbon.

The winner of the Santa's Reindeer Pet Contest was a Yorkie wearing plush stuffed antlers with a couple of jingle bells attached. It might not sound like much, but the antlers stood over two feet high. The dog stood eight inches high, tops.

"That was fun." I bumped Bea's hip as we walked. "Are you bringing Peanut Butter back to the café?"

"No. He's had enough excitement for today. I'll meet you back there. Don't tell my mom who won. I want to see her face when you describe that little dog."

I nodded and laughed with Treacle dozing in my arms. As Bea went one way and I went the other, I was shocked to see a group of teenagers bouncing and pogoing excitedly around one person. It was Mr. Clyde Tumble. What kind of cologne could he be wearing that attracted teenagers that way? They were shouting hellos and Merry Christmases. Clyde was high-fiving them and giving side hugs and pats on the back to his adoring fans.

I thought back to my high school days and recalled my favorite teacher, Miss Arndt. She taught English, and I just had a knack for the subject, so I did receive a little favoritism in the class, but I never acted like this when I saw her in public. Seeing a teacher outside school was like spotting a skunk. You acknowledge it's there then quickly hurry in any other direction.

But Mr. Tumble was a rock star.

"Will you be at school after break?" one especially bubbly girl asked with her ponytail swinging wildly behind her.

"Yes," Mr. Tumble replied. "The superintendent has hired me on full time."

"That's great!" she and her friends squealed. "Got

to go, Mr. Tumble. Merry Christmas!" And half a dozen more Merry Christmases were shouted as the crowd dispersed.

After Mr. Tumble waved good-bye, he turned around and instantly saw me. I smiled warily and nodded since my arms were full of kitty.

"Well, this is a nice surprise." He strolled up to me as if he suspected I might have been following him.

"Hi, Mr. Tumble."

"*Let's get out of here.*" Treacle's claws dug into my coat. "*Something is up.*"

"Please, call me Clyde. Mr. Tumble is my father."

"Sure." I squeezed Treacle to try and calm him down. "I've heard that one before." I looked down at my cat and saw his eyes were wide and alert. He'd caught a whiff of something nearby.

"Yeah, it's not a great joke."

"Was that a joke?" The words just fell out of my mouth, but Clyde didn't seem at all insulted. It wasn't that I was trying to insult him. On the contrary. My ability to make small talk was being seriously handicapped by my introversion and my cat pushing his body further and further into my chest.

"Ha. Well, I wouldn't dream of quitting my day job," he replied, never taking his eyes from mine.

"I'm a teacher. Those were some of my students." He jerked his thumb in the direction of the mob of boys and girls who had just left. "I was just a substitute, but I've been hired on full time. Just in the nick of time, too. A Christmas miracle of sorts."

"What school will you be teaching at?" I asked while trying to shift Treacle. He was having none of that. All four sets of claws were attached to my coat.

"Something is wrong! I need to leave! We need to get out of here!"

"Bibich High School," he answered enthusiastically as he reached to pet Treacle, who let out a deep and threatening growl from the pit of his gut. *"She can't hear you, but I can. Run, kitty!"*

Before I knew what was happening, Treacle leaped from my arms, down onto the sidewalk, and darted madly in between the legs of the other pedestrians. I looked around but didn't see Treacle, nor did I know where that menacing voice had come from.

"I don't know what's gotten into my cat," I said. "I had him in the reindeer contest. He's probably just tired and cranky from being on display." I took a few nervous steps in the direction my cat had shot off in. "Did you hear something? Like someone yelling?"

Clyde shrugged and shook his head. "Would you

like me to help you find him?" Clyde stepped dangerously close to me, and for a moment, I thought he was going to try and kiss me. The worst part was I was afraid I might have just let him.

"Oh, no," I insisted and casually rocked back on my heel to put a little distance between us. "He'll find his way home. So you're at Bibich. Is that why you were at the football game?"

"I didn't think you noticed me."

I blushed like an idiot.

"So, Cath Greenstone. When are you going to let me take you out?" He smiled, and I noticed his teeth were perfectly even. He really was easy on the eyes.

"I told you before that I have a boyfriend."

"Well, that's fine, but it isn't what I asked." He shifted from one foot to the other, and as he looked at me, a couple of strands of his hair curled over his forehead.

"I wanted to know when you were going to let me take you out. That has nothing to do with your boyfriend." He blinked innocently.

I was sure the temperature in the air was going up, because suddenly I was getting hot beneath my peacoat.

"I have to go." I smiled. "I'm due back at work. It was nice to see you again, Clyde."

"Don't think I'm giving up, Cath Greenstone." He took my hand in his and brought it to his lips. "I don't mind a game of cat and mouse."

The fever spread by that kiss on my hand was deadly. I don't know if the guy practiced on melons or something, but he certainly had a way with women. The worst part was that a little bit of me, maybe just the first knuckle of my baby toe, was enjoying the attention and wanting to ponder the what-if scenarios. The rest of me wanted to focus on Tom. But you'd be surprised at how influential the pinky toe can be.

"I'll be seeing you." He leaned over. Once again, I thought he was going to kiss me, but he didn't. He stuffed his hands in his pockets and began to whistle "Jingle Bells" as he strolled away, turning to look at me again and smiling deviously.

A strange feeling settled into my stomach. I was attracted to Clyde Tumble, no doubt. But I couldn't stop thinking he had a sort of sleazy, even a greasy quality to him like a thin layer of sweat. But it wasn't sweat. He smelled really good, and his skin was perfectly smooth and clear. His clothes were neat and in traditional dude styles. But I wondered if he took off his coat and rolled up his sleeves that he wouldn't have amateur prison tattoos of spiderwebs on his elbows and the names of his three illegitimate children written in some weird calligraphy on his forearms.

"It's just nerves, Cath," I muttered as I turned to continue toward the café. "How often do you get a guy like that flirting with you? Or any guy, for that matter."

I knew that I didn't usually arrange my face in the most welcoming expression, not because I was angry. I was just usually thinking deep thoughts. Okay, maybe not *deep* thoughts about world peace, but they were my thoughts and serious enough to have me focused as I walk down the sidewalk. No one would look at me and think, *Now there is a girl who looks chatty. I think I'll go have a pleasant conversation with her*.

When I was back at the Brew-Ha-Ha, Treacle was not.

"It's not terribly cold out there," my aunt said to ease my worry. "He has a fur coat and knows how to keep warm until he's ready to come home."

"It was bizarre." I tied an apron around my waist and stepped behind the counter to wash the huge mountain of dishes from the lunchtime rush. "Treacle was fine. A total gentleman through the whole reindeer contest, and he let lots of people pet him and stroke his head. Then we're walking, and suddenly he says we have to get out of there. Before I could say a word, he jumped out of my arms and shot off like a bullet. I thought he'd meet me back here, but there's no sign of him."

Just then, Bea walked in the shop.

"The more I think about it, the more I think that contest was rigged." Bea pouted while pulling off her coat and scarf. She looked from me to her mom and back. "Did you tell her about the dog that won?"

"Not yet." I leaned on the counter. "I ran into Clyde Tumble on the way here. My cat took off unexpectedly, too. He wasn't at your house, was he?"

"No, honey." Bea batted her eyes. "But what did Mr. Tumble have to say?"

I rolled my shoulders and blushed while I smirked at her.

"He still wants to take me to dinner. But I'm not interested."

"Are you sure?" Aunt Astrid straightened the papers and snapped a rubber band around the bulky stack.

"Yeah. There's something about him. I know he's handsome, but I don't think going out with him would be a good idea."

"Well, that's up to you. You know best when it

comes your love life." Aunt Astrid smiled. It was annoying because she had that same devious smile on her face that Clyde seemed to have. It was as if she didn't believe I didn't want to go out with him any more than he did.

"Yeah," I grumbled. "I do."

Radio Station

❧❧❧

After closing the café just as the sky went from purple to black, I hurried to my house to find my cat. The temperature had dropped, and I was worried about him waiting outside for me for too long. But when I got there, Treacle was nowhere to be found.

I banged on Bea's door. Normally, I wouldn't worry about him, but he bolted so suddenly that afternoon. Something had really scared him, and that wasn't like Treacle.

"No. I haven't seen him," she said, pulling on a thick, fuzzy wool sweater.

"Peanut Butter. Did you see Treacle at all today?"

"No. Is he all right?"

"I don't know." I wrung my hands. "I'm going to

go check with your mom. Maybe Marshmallow's seen him."

"I'm going with you." Bea grabbed her keys and then scooped Peanut Butter into one arm. She slipped the other through mine. We hurried to my aunt's home. We let ourselves in with Bea's key.

"Treacle didn't come home. Do you know…" Before I could say another word, I saw the black bundle on a pillow in front of the fireplace.

"*I'm here,*" he loudly meowed.

"*Where in the world did you run off to? I've been worried sick.*" I walked over and scooped up the animal. "*You just jumped out of my arms and ran away. What was that all about, Treacle?*"

"*Didn't you hear him?*" he asked.

"*Hear who?*" I asked.

Aunt Astrid and Bea talked between themselves as I gave Treacle my utmost attention.

"*The man you were talking with. Didn't you hear him threaten me?*"

"*I heard something garbled. I thought it was just some residual paranormal gunk from something that happened at another time.*" I stroked his head.

"What's wrong?" My aunt could tell by the way I was looking at Treacle that we were discussing something important.

"When I was bringing Treacle back to the café, we ran into Clyde. I thought I heard something in my head. Another voice, but you know, I've learned over the years that sometimes that happens." I shrugged as I looked at my aunt and cousin. "Sometimes my thoughts get loud or explode into view like a popping balloon. Sometimes I'll pick up the internal ramblings of a dog barking at me while I'm crossing the sidewalk. We were around a lot of pets today, and I guess when Treacle and I were walking alone, I didn't realize it should have been quieter. I'm so sorry."

"*But you did hear him?*" Treacle put his paw on my chest.

"*Yes.* 'She can't hear you, but I can.' *That's what he said, right?*" My whole body began to shake. "The voice I heard was choppy and sort of like a radio station that didn't come in clearly. Maybe that's why I didn't link it to Clyde at first."

The whole room was quiet as Bea and Aunt Astrid looked at Treacle and me.

"I'm not following. How come you can hear Clyde's thoughts?" Bea asked.

I looked down at Treacle.

"*Please don't tell me I've been gifted with hearing human thoughts, now, too,*" I whined. "*The last thing I want to know is what humans are thinking, especially if it concerns me."*

"I don't think that is it," Treacle assured me. *"I think Clyde is the other cat."*

"The *other* cat?" I barked out loud. "Who is the first cat?"

"That would be Mr. Wayne." Aunt Astrid pointed to me as if I'd just won something. "He still had issues with the children at the school. Let's not forget the portal we found in *his* house. That is a pretty good indicator that even if he isn't the first Diabolus Formarum Catus, which I'm sure he was, he was definitely in cahoots with them."

"So why does Clyde want to hurt my cat?" I asked, suddenly feeling angry that the big bully scared Treacle but tried to sweet-talk me.

"Remember, Cath." My aunt looked at me with eyes that burned with an intense internal fire. "We are Greenstones. The bloodline that destroyed the great-great-great grand-pappy of this creature. It knows what we are and who we are and that we are stronger with our Familiars than with each other at times. Do away with the gatekeeper, and you have full access to the kingdom."

"I don't like being compared to a castle being stormed," I replied, wrinkling my nose. "That comment you made has all kinds of double meanings, and I just feel dirty repeating it."

"Who said anything about storming a castle?" my aunt sputtered. "I'm saying the Diabolus Formarum Catus will divide and conquer any way it can. It came after me when I was alone. It blustered after you when you were walking by yourself and may have accomplished its goal had Treacle not been there, too."

"What about me?" Bea asked. "Do I have cooties or something?"

"Yes," I answered, shaking my head sadly.

"No. But you've been either with me, with Cath, with both of us, or in your home behind locked doors," Aunt Astrid observed. She finally put the food out, but suddenly I wasn't all that hungry. Okay, I was a little hungry. But I chewed slowly and barely tasted the food.

"That would explain why I could hear him. But he doesn't *know* that I can. If his true form is a cat and he maneuvers around as a human, I can pick up his thoughts," I said. "But these cats, you guys still say there are two of them, right?" I looked at Treacle, Marshmallow, and Peanut Butter. They all agreed that yes, there were definitely two of them that they had either heard about or seen. "These cats are mean, right? They aren't just using this dimension to get from one place to another. They are up to something."

"Mr. Wayne isn't up to too much anymore." Bea shrugged as she pulled a container of hummus from the fridge. "Being he's dead and all."

Before I could comment on anything, the front door opened, and a gust of cold wind shot in behind it.

"I thought I'd find you here." Jake walked into the kitchen and up to Bea to give her a kiss on the cheek then gave one to Aunt Astrid as well. I high-fived him then turned to Blake, who was a few steps behind him. He looked cold and rather annoyed.

"Are you all right?" I asked Blake. "You look more perturbed than usual." I know it wasn't a very Christmassy salutation, but we were dealing with Blake Samberg here. Mister I Don't Believe in Witches but I'll Date Darla Castellano.

"It's the Gale Wayne situation," Blake muttered then looked me in the eyes. "We found something so strange that I don't even know what to think. Tell me what you think about this."

Burnam

❧❧❧

As Bea put on a pot of coffee and Aunt Astrid pulled out some more food, I took a seat and listened to the story of what Blake and Jake had found.

After Mr. Wayne was taken to the police station for questioning, the uniformed police officers still at his home conducted a search. Each room was meticulously scoured and searched for any trace evidence that Bruce Lyle or Donna Flint had been there. Starting with the bedroom, they searched every drawer, underneath the bed, and in the closets. The bathroom, the office, the living room, and the garage were gone over with a magnifying glass and a fine-tooth comb.

"It wasn't until they found what was under the

sink that this whole situation went sideways." Blake looked at Jake, who nodded in agreement.

"My gosh." Bea wrinkled her nose. "What did they find?"

"Anything put underneath a sink can't be good," I added.

"It was just a small bag," Blake replied. "Like the kind big enough for a sandwich. But it had a barrette in it. There was hair still attached, and blood."

"A trophy," I exclaimed. "That's what that is. He kept a trophy. Was that Donna Flint's barrette?"

"No." Blake shook his head and squinted as he looked at Jake.

"After we submitted it for testing and asked the Flints if the barrette was Donna's, we found out that not only was it *not* Donna's, but it was actually from a girl who disappeared over three years ago," Jake said. "An unsolved cold case but not in Wonder Falls. This victim lived in Burnam."

"Burnam is almost three hours away." Bea poured two cups of coffee then looked at me, raising the pot. I shook my head no. The last thing I needed at the moment was an additional stimulant. "And it isn't the safest town to live in."

"No. It isn't," Jake said. "High crime. High poverty. Also, a high number of runaways. Our victim with the barrette ran away from home at around this time of year, and her body was found in the same shape as Bruce and Donna's. We think Mr. Wayne was much more careful in his murdering at first. As he got bolder, he came closer to home."

"But you said you didn't find any evidence of Bruce or Donna at his home," Aunt Astrid said as she stared into the darkness outside the window. "Bruce was found near the storage facility, but Donna was killed somewhere else before ultimately landing in his storage facility. I know it's a stretch, but could it be a setup?"

"I suppose," Jake said.

"I'm glad you said that, Astrid." Blake slapped the counter. "Something has me thinking the exact same thing."

"I don't see how it can be possible." Jake shook his head then took a sip of his coffee. "Who would have chosen Mr. Gale Wayne, high school teacher from Wonder Falls, who was a bachelor and had no family, no social life to speak of, and no enemies list that anyone could come up with?"

"I'm not saying I've got it all figured out," Blake said. "I'm saying something is rubbing me the wrong way about this. I'm thinking there are too many loose ends that, if threaded back together, will project a very different picture."

"It's just too hard to face." Jake stood stock-still. "We have to accept the fact that we had a killer living not just among us, but teaching our children every day for years before he was finally brought into the light."

Bea put her hand on Jake's shoulder.

"To be honest, I'm glad he did the dirty work for us," he continued. "He took his reasons and his methods to the grave with him. No one will know why or how, and we're all better off for it."

The room got awfully quiet, and I looked at Bea, who shook her head before quietly suggesting Jake go upstairs to take a hot shower and wash off the day's residue.

"Blake, you are welcome to stay overnight. The guest room could always use a little company," Bea suggested.

"No. Thanks, Bea." He looked frustrated all over again. "There will be a briefing early tomorrow morning, and the weather station determined we'll get a light sprinkling of snow. It would be best if my old jalopy rests inside the garage tonight. Most cars experience trouble when the temperature dips below thirty degrees. The older the model, the more trouble you can expect."

"Detective," Aunt Astrid said, "would you be so kind as to walk my niece home? Could you take just a minute to make sure she gets home safely?"

Blake looked down at me without expression then back up at my aunt. With about as much enthusiasm as a man in for a root canal, Blake accepted my aunt's request.

"It's just to be on the safe side." She looked at me sternly.

"It's okay, Blake." I slid off the stool and shook my head while grabbing a few more slices of lunch meat, bread, and cheese to take with me on the long journey across the street to my home. "I can manage by myself."

"No. Your aunt is right," Blake said. "The last week before Christmas always ramps up in violent assaults and robberies. Too many office parties with too many open bars and too much excitement. This is also the time that DUIs and deaths due to drunk driving go off the charts. The death tolls don't even include the suicide rate that…"

"Thanks for those fascinating facts," I blurted out. "Nothing like crime stats to put you in the Christmas mood." I grabbed my coat and patted my thigh for Treacle to join us. Before leaving, I kissed Aunt Astrid and Bea on the cheek, clapped Jake on the back, and looked up at Blake.

"I don't need a babysitter," I mumbled.

Blake didn't say a word but nodded and said good night to my family as he followed behind me.

Once outside, the cold wrapped me up in its grip, and I was shivering underneath my open coat. My legs quickly hustled down the porch steps to the sidewalk. Blake was tall, and two of my steps equaled one of his.

"So have you gotten your Christmas shopping done?" I asked in order to break the uncomfortable silence that had settled over us.

"Most of it. I don't have that many people to buy for."

"Well, that's a Christmas miracle in itself," I said encouragingly. I wasn't sure why, but I didn't want him to feel bad. No matter how lousy he made me feel. How crazy was that? "Some people just go so crazy buying gadgets and junk that will be broken or forgotten in a matter of days. I like homemade gifts. No matter how bad they turn out, you can see the love that was put into them, you know?"

"I don't remember the last time I received a homemade gift," Blake mused, and I could have sworn I saw a smile on his face. Or at least the slight curling of the right corner of his mouth. That was darn near hysterics where Blake Samberg was concerned.

"I'm surprised you can remember the last time you didn't get coal. How long ago was *that*?" I joked.

This was the season of good will toward men. If I couldn't be decent at this time of year, I really wasn't fit to exist the other eleven months. Plus, the smile that spread across Blake's lips was worth it. I had to laugh out loud.

"I'll have you know that I never got coal."

"Never?" I shook my head. "See, lying is what gets you coal. Santa is listening."

Once on my porch, I quickly pulled out my keys and unlocked the front door, flipping on the light in the foyer and letting Treacle race inside.

"You'll be all right?" Blake asked.

"Yeah." I nodded and made sure I didn't look at Blake's handsome face for too long. "Thanks for the armed escort. I'll take it from here."

"Will you and Tom be attending the Christmas party?" he asked before I stepped inside.

"Yeah. It's a pretty big deal. He's wearing his dress uniform, and I've got to figure out something for myself. You're going, too, right?"

Blake nodded as he looked behind him.

"Do you have a date?" The words came out softly, as I intended. There was no need to be snooty or rude. I wanted to know for selfish reasons, and the guilt that I wanted to know was enough for me to mind my tongue.

"There's someone I have in mind. I haven't asked her yet."

"Well, you better, pal. It's getting late. A girl has to have a couple days' notice in order to get all primped and preened in time for the big event." I smirked, as I assumed it would be Darla Castellano he'd be taking. I'd feel like an English bulldog next to a French poodle no matter what I wore.

"Thanks for the advice."

"My pleasure." I stepped across the threshold and turned around. "Be careful going home."

"Have a nice evening, Cath."

I smiled before shutting the door. As I leaned against it, I let out my breath and looked down at Treacle.

"That took a long time," he purred.

"Yeah. I'm trying to be nice. Is that wrong?"

"Not at all. I find you irresistible." He gave me a forceful head-butt and a snug leg rub before looking up at me and whipping his tail.

"*Right back at you, kitty.*" I bent down and picked him up in my arms. "So what do you think of this Diabolus Formarum Catus business?"

"*I'm not sure what to think.*"

"Well, I think I have a plan. Why don't you and I discuss it before we present it to the rest of the coven? You can help me iron out all the details."

"*Yes, let's discuss over a saucer of milk and maybe some tuna fish.*"

"*Oh yes, and I still have some of Aunt Astrid's snacks in my pockets. Come on. Let's get to work.*"

Feliz Navidad

❧✿❧

"**A**bsolutely not!" Bea yelled as she opened the blinds at the café the next day. "It is too dangerous, and I'm saying no."

"Bea, it's the only way to get to the bottom of this," I replied. "Besides, we have the element of surprise. He doesn't know my gift. We could use that to our advantage."

"It would require you be alone with that monster. *If* he is the monster. Whether he is or not, he's in some cahoots with something dark, and I'm not letting you go off by yourself into what could be a trap."

"Aunt Astrid." I turned my back to Bea and looked at her. "I'm the one he's trying to get to go out with him. It's only logical that I accept, alone, and see what I can find out."

"I can't see an upside to you going off alone," Aunt Astrid said. "But what do you think of having him come here first?"

"You don't think it will seem suspicious?" I asked.

"That's a good idea, Mom." Bea stepped forward and put her hands on my hips to scoot me to the side while she slipped behind the counter. "Have him come here, and I'll shake his hand politely and get a read on him."

"That's a good call, Bea." Aunt Astrid winked at her daughter. "No. I don't think it would look suspicious at all. It would just look like a young woman having her family meet the guy taking her on their first date."

"What will you do once he's here?" I scoffed. "You know he isn't going to offer up any information with all three of us here. In fact, having all of us in one place might work to his benefit. With one fell swoop, he could have us all pushing up daisies before we could say Feliz Navidad."

"Nope." Aunt Astrid shook her head. "All we need to do is cloak the café in a mirage spell. He'll see the café the way we want him to. As soon as he steps through the door, he'll see what we want him to see. Bea can do her reading, and I'll bind him until we find out if he's really the shape-shifter we suspect he is or if he's just a man. If he's just a man, I'm sure he'll never want to see you again after this whole ordeal, so no need to discuss with Tom."

"Right?" I covered my face with my hands and ran them through my hair. "How am I ever going to explain to Tom what I'm doing? He'll never go for it. He might be the most understanding boyfriend since Jake embraced his wife's empathic abilities. But I don't think that extends to making dates with other guys who are suspected killer shape-shifters."

"He knows what a sting is, right?" Bea asked.

"Of course. But how do you think Jake would feel if you were putting yourself out there to attract a killer?" I pursed my lips. "See why I need to do this alone? I'll take a protection spell. That will be enough."

"How are you going to get in touch with him?" Aunt Astrid asked.

I hadn't thought of that. But an idea quickly came to me that was almost as dangerous as the date itself.

"He works at Bibich High School," I mumbled.

"You can't just walk onto school property," Bea said. "They'll have you tossed in the clink for sure."

"Right. But I could follow him when he leaves.

I've done stakeouts before."

"You sat in a car with Blake for an hour or so. That's doesn't really make you an expert in the surveillance arena," Bea teased.

"Right," I agreed. "Not like you when you sat outside the Whole Foods for ten hours, waiting for the new quinoa shipment to drop."

"No." Aunt Astrid startled us out of our ribbing. "School's out for the Christmas break. Anyway, it's much too dangerous. Look, we aren't in a huge hurry. When we close the café, we can find the right spell for the right option that will get us the same result. That is, getting him to show up here."

I shrugged but wasn't ready to wait until tonight to *maybe* find a safe route to lure Clyde to the café for an aura reading and possible binding spell.

This thing was a child killer. If we waited and another child went missing, how would I ever forgive myself? Teenagers are an absolute terror. I know that. But they deserve the right to grow up and look back at their teenage years and cringe at their stupidity and ignorance just like the rest of us.

When the morning crowd had finally wound down, I decided I needed to get a little fresh air and see if I could find a Christmas gift for Tom.

"Still no luck with that?" Bea asked.

"Nope." I shook my head. "I'm starting to get desperate."

"Well, I still say you can't go wrong with getting him some music," Bea said.

"You might be right," I mumbled. "But I'm going to give it one last try. I'll be back in about an hour."

Once I was behind the wheel of my car, I directed it in the direction of Mr. Wayne's house and hit the gas. Something in my gut said that maybe I'd find Clyde around this area.

When I pulled up outside the house, parking in almost the same spot I had just a few days earlier with Aunt Astrid and Bea, I saw the yellow police tape flapping lazily in the breeze. It was draped across the porch and along part of the driveway, but what had been across the door was either not taped down securely enough or had been pulled away by someone wanting to get in—or out—of the house.

I cut the engine and just waited.

There was no car in the driveway. Mr. Wayne's car had probably been towed to the station to be scoured for evidence. The curtains were drawn. I cracked my car window and took a deep breath of cold air to wake myself up.

"What are you doing, Cath?" I muttered, looking behind me in the rearview mirror. "You aren't going to find anything or see anything. Clyde isn't dumb enough to come and hang around the house of a murderer."

That was when I noticed something. I often saw things out of the corners of my eyes. Aunt Astrid said it was the spirits of the Greenstone family cats long gone keeping an eye on me. Bea said it was my mother keeping an eye on me. I often thought it was just a trick of the light or an overactive imagination. But what I was looking at was none of these things.

Without blinking, I sat in the driver's seat and stared at the landscape in front of me. Of course I thought perhaps I had the pleasure of witnessing a mole burrowing under the ground causing the grass to "breathe" up and down, but the area appearing to "breathe" expanded until it was the size of a Volkswagen. Too big for a mole, for sure.

I blinked, even squeezed my eyes shut and opened them again, expecting to see that it was my own untrustworthy peepers that were watering and causing the illusion of movement.

But the more I watched, the more I knew it was neither of these things. Every couple of seconds, a shimmering line would flash. Sometimes it looked like a hunched back. Sometimes it looked like a haunch. Sometimes it looked like a row of ribs.

There are creatures in the sea, way down deep, that are translucent and for all intents and purposes invisible until a diver or a camera is right up on them. Then their outline can be clearly seen. This was the same thing.

I watched as it moved down the street and up the grass to Mr. Wayne's empty house. The grass surrendered to four invisible feet that pressed it into the ground before it disappeared completely from my view.

"You don't want to go, Cath," I muttered. "You don't because an invisible enemy has all the advantage."

I nodded but thought, *Just a peek. A peek through the window wouldn't harm anything. I've got the element of surprise on my side. Take that, superpower of invisibility.*

Before I could talk myself out of it, I was out of the car and traipsing up the grass, following alongside the footprints only I could see at this point since the grass was slowly and stiffly arching back to its original position.

By the time I reached the front porch, my breath sounded as though I had been swimming laps without coming up for air until I was nearly drowned. That was when I noticed the noises around me had also stopped.

Creature

❧

"Just a quick peek. Just casually stroll around the side of the house and peek inside like you're looking for someone you know."

I stretched my neck, and with my arms swinging as if I were going to war, I marched around the opposite side of the house as though I owned the place.

The first window was into the bedroom, but the blinds were drawn tightly. No use trying to get a glimpse in there. I continued, looking behind me once, twice before I came to the bathroom.

This could be a misdemeanor, I thought while turning my head left then right to make sure the coast was clear. I looked inside. It was empty. "Thank goodness."

As I made my way to the back of the house, my

nerves had calmed. It was almost as though in those last few steps I forgot exactly what I was looking for.

"It's an invisible thing, Cath. Don't forget," I whispered. The next window led to the kitchen. It was then that I wondered if the mirage-causing thing was even on the first level of the house. It might have preferred the privacy of the basement, the windows of which I was standing directly in front of. I froze.

Just as I was about to run, I heard a clatter from the kitchen area. I quickly stepped to the right and pressed my back firmly against the brick of the building while holding my breath.

Just then, the woman from the house next door came outside onto her porch. She stepped into what looked like a closet, but as I squinted and studied the tall cabinet, I realized it was a portable sauna. Next to that was a bubbling cauldron of a hot tub. I wondered how many times she had come down with pneumonia, stepping outside in the middle of December in her bathing suit.

Getting back to the task at hand, I carefully and quietly inched my way to the kitchen window. There were plain white blinds pulled down but slanted open just enough for me to peek inside.

At first it was dark. But as my eyes adjusted and I

held my breath, I heard something grunting. My heart froze. I needed to block out the glare from the sun against the window to focus on what I thought I was seeing inside.

The creature slowly began to appear. It writhed and squirmed like a maggot that had fallen on hot pavement, with a sickly yellowish-pink color rippling across its mass. It reminded me of a cat trying to expel a hairball as it jerked and hacked, rolling its appendages, growling and hissing as its metamorphosis continued.

I tried to focus, but the blinds obstructed my view as if they were railroad ties. Stretching up on my tiptoes gave me a better glimpse, but due to the fact that I am not an expert in surveillance, I didn't observe the lifted screen window that was barely on the track. When I pushed myself up on my tiptoes, the window frame was taxed. Down came the screen window with a crash on the back of my neck.

Now, screen windows are not heavy. Decapitation was not a possibility. However, disembowelment by a slowly materializing catlike monster was within the realm of possibility. At least, in my mind I assumed it was.

My hair had fallen over my face, my jacket had gotten hung up, and before I pulled my head and the screen out of the window, the beast had slinked up to the glass on the other side. Obviously, the blinds caused it some problems seeing as well, because one bony claw slipped through the slats and tore the entire fixture from its attachments in the frame.

I reeled backward, my right leg tripping over my left, to land on my backside. All the air in my lungs was knocked out in an unladylike grunt. I kicked and scurried backward on my hands and feet as the thing in the kitchen grew and grew until its massive head and shoulders took up the entire window.

At first its eyes were downcast, and I thought that maybe I was in luck and the sun affected its vision. But it snapped its head up at me, hissing as it scratched at the glass with its skeletal claws. Its eyes were yellow pinpricks in a sea of black.

As the hairless cat scratched at the windowsill, I scrambled to my feet. But the thing wasn't scratching at the glass. It was fumbling with the safety latches. I heard them both snap as they were released, and the window flew up, nearly cracking the frame. I did the only thing I could do. I screamed.

"I know who you are! I know who you are! You'll suffer! You and the other members of your family will suffer for decades upon decades!"

I screamed again as it started to crawl out the window toward me, but thank heaven for the weird lady next door who was just trying to enjoy her sauna in December. She threw the little cedar door open with enough force to rattle the whole closet and looked in my direction.

Yours truly stared back at the window and watched with disgust as the enormous cat retreated back inside the dark house. Wasting no time, I got to my feet and took off running toward the front yard and my car.

The driver's-side door wasn't even closed before the engine was running and I had the accelerator pressed to the floor. Tires squealing, I peeled out of there and didn't dare look in the rearview mirror until I was well meshed with the daily lunch traffic on the road.

Brushing my hair out of my face and trying to smooth it out with one trembling hand, I wondered if I should say anything to my aunt and cousin. Did they need to know what I did? Did they need to know that I saw that thing and that it saw me? And what it said? The awful threat it screamed in my head?

If Clyde was that cat or talked to that cat or had

anything to do with the giant hairless cats, there was no way he would agree to meet with me now.

"I don't know if he recognized me," I mumbled as I looked in the rearview mirror again. My hair was a mess. "It looks like I had a wild tryst." Bea was certainly going to have something to say about my appearance, for sure.

I decided I was going to have to tell them I went to investigate on my own and it turned out horribly, horribly wrong.

⚜

"ARE YOU OUT OF YOUR MIND?" BEA CRIED, causing two ladies who had been deep in their conversation to stop and turn in our direction.

"Apparently," I said and sighed as I pulled off my coat.

"Cath, why do you take such crazy chances?" Bea rushed around the counter and took me in her arms, giving me a tight squeeze. "You could have gotten hurt or even worse. Do you think it saw you? Maybe it followed you."

"I know. I don't know. Maybe?" I sulked. When my aunt came from the kitchen and looked at the two of us, it was apparent by her expression that she knew something was up.

"What did you do, Cath?"

Thankfully, Bea pleaded my defense and really put quite a spin on my whole debacle, reminding my aunt that this gave us a good bit more information than we had before and that we were going to have to check into the Wayne house sooner or later. By the time she was done, I was feeling downright proud, and Aunt Astrid's glare was quickly melting into a smirk.

"Well, Bea is right about one thing." My aunt brushed my long hair behind my shoulder. "You certainly did show great bravery. Or could it have been stupidity?"

"Maybe a little of both," I said.

As the afternoon became evening, and after the sun had totally disappeared behind the horizon, we experienced a little lull in foot traffic.

"So tell us a little more about what exactly you saw," my aunt urged me.

Making a Scene

B y the time I finished relaying every detail of my harrowing experience, it was pitch black outside and a few flurries had started to waft around.

"Well, whatever this Diabolus Formarum Catus is doing, it likes to do it from the Wayne house." Aunt Astrid held her tarot card deck in her hands and shuffled it casually as we discussed our options. "Sadly, we may have to go back there. But we can be better prepared this time."

"For sure." I walked over to the right storefront window to pull up the blinds.

Someone had obviously closed them to block out the afternoon sun that sometimes temporarily blinded a person. "I'm thinking maybe a nice invisibility spell along with a teleportation spell, and maybe you can fix it so I shoot electricity out of my fingernails. Bea can't be trusted with such power. Give her the ability to throw her voice. That's a good one."

"Oh, I can be trusted," Bea snapped as she rolled her eyes at me.

Still giggling, I grabbed the string for the blinds and gave them a yank. There, standing behind the glass, staring in at me, was Clyde Tumble. I let out a totally embarrassing yelp. After putting my hand over my heart and looking up at the ceiling, I waved at him without smiling.

Before I could catch my breath, he was waving to me to come outside. He looked bashful, as if he were a high school boy trying to woo a girl while her mother and father were standing behind her.

I pinched my eyebrows together and mouthed the words, *It's cold out there*.

"Cath, get him to come in, and I'll make him a special tea. We'll see what's going on inside that very handsome head of his." Bea pretended to look over her mother's shoulder at her tarot cards.

I smiled as pleasantly as I could and waved for him to come in. But he thrust his hands in his pockets and jerked his head for me to go outside.

"I don't think he's falling for it," I muttered as I

went for my coat. As I pulled it from behind the counter, the chimes over the door went off, and Clyde was leaning his head inside.

"Cath. Come take a quick walk with me."

"Hi, Clyde," I answered rather loudly. "Come on in and meet my family."

Without crossing the threshold, Clyde waved, said a quick howdy, then pulled his head back outside, letting the door close behind him.

"Well, if he isn't the Diabolus Formarum Catus, he has the manners of a 1700s Romanian thaumaturge," Aunt Astrid muttered.

"I'll be back in a minute." I flipped my hair out of the collar of my coat and stepped toward the door.

"I don't think you should go." My cousin touched my arm. "Not by yourself."

"What can he do?" I looked from Bea to my aunt. "It's busy out there with last-minute shoppers, and there is plenty of light from the streetlamps. He won't do anything. I'll be fine and see what I can find out. Knowledge is power. Isn't that what GI Joe always said?"

"Now isn't the time to seek sage advice from a cartoon soldier." Bea looked sternly at me. "Tell him to come back later."

"It will look suspicious." I grumbled as if I were

having a real hard time putting on my mittens. "Look, I'll stay in front of the café. That way you can keep an eye on me."

"Heaven knows you need that." Bea folded her arms in front of her and looked suspiciously out the window at Clyde, who was looking at her and Aunt Astrid then back to the people passing by.

I walked outside, setting off the wind chimes that hung from the door, and for an unknown reason, it reminded me of funeral glockenspiels instead of just the pretty tinkling of metal chimes. I shook my head and rubbed my arms against the cold.

"Hi."

"Thanks for coming out to meet me," Clyde purred. "Walk with me."

"What?" I smiled and blinked as if my IQ had suddenly dropped to the floor and I didn't understand his words.

"Take a walk with me." He slipped his arm around mine and began to gently guide me down the sidewalk. "Let's talk."

"Sure," I agreed pleasantly. "I love to talk. In fact, my boyfriend says I have something to say about everything. I don't know if that's good or not. My whole life, I've been told I talk too much. Unfortunately, I don't really have a filter. That's too bad. Bea does. My cousin, Bea, is like a picture-perfect example of a lady. She really is. That's probably why we get along so well because we are such opposites."

I was rambling, letting the words fall out of my mouth like tumbleweeds skittering across the desert. Something was not right, and I felt a dread in the very center of my chest. I never use the word dread. But this was unequivocally dread.

As I looked around, I expected to see that thing that was in the kitchen of the Wayne house, but all I saw were Christmas shoppers and a couple of carolers and a few couples walking hand in hand. I was talking, but I barely heard what I was saying as my eyes flitted around, looking for the doom I was sure was creeping up on me.

"Have you gotten your Christmas shopping done?" I continued. "I've got just a few more things to buy. I don't know when I'll be able to get to it. It might be better to wait until the day after when everything goes on sale. Right? Not a bad idea."

"You seem nervous." Clyde's voice was velvety. His eyes were clear and sparkly, and I was sure I could see the snowflakes falling reflected in them.

"Oh, no," I lied. "I'm just talkative."

"I think you should shut your flapping mouth," Clyde whispered to me as his grip tightened around my arm. "We can do this quickly, but if you try and fight me, I'll make it very uncomfortable for you."

"What are you talking about?" I played dumb.

"I know who you are...Greenstone." He grinned at me like a devil. His handsome face contorted into the mask of a gargoyle before my eyes. "Your family has caused me decades of pain. It's time to return the favor."

"What?" I tried to claw his fingers from my arm, but they were clamped down too tightly. "I'm not sure what you're talking about. There's got to be at least a hundred Greenstones in the world. Are you sure you have the right one? I'm sure there are a couple of weirdoes in the family tree living in Wisconsin or Nebraska that might fit your bill a little better. Have you checked that out?"

"You're not making your situation any better," he growled.

"I don't believe that," I protested.

"Cath?" There it was, that voice that brought with it the feeling of dread. Now I agreed with Clyde that my situation wasn't getting better.

"Tom?" I whirled around and saw him walking slowly up behind me as if he were approaching a coiled-up rattlesnake. "What are you doing here?"

"I stopped by the café, and your aunt and cousin

said they didn't know where you'd gone." He looked skeptically at Clyde, and I could tell he didn't like him instantly. There was no cordiality, as there was with Blake Samberg. These two guys would not be standing around, shooting the breeze over a couple of beers, that was obvious. "So...here you are."

I swallowed hard. Looking at Clyde, I tried to pull my arm away casually but to no avail.

"Yeah, um, I'm just taking a stroll with my friend Clyde." I had to get Tom out of here. My heart began to break as I imagined the only way I could chase him away. "I mean, that's okay, right?"

"What?" Tom looked at me, and I could feel the weight of his disappointment settle on my bones like a metal coating. "Cath, would you mind if I talked to you alone for just a second?"

"You're not going to make a scene, are you?" The words were like nails scraping out of my mouth. I could see the confusion and hurt on his face. But he had to get out of there. He might have accepted me as his witchy-woman, but I couldn't risk him getting hurt or worse by this man-creature. He had to leave. "I'll call you maybe."

Tom stared at me before snapping his eyes toward Clyde. I saw them focus on his fingers around my arm. It didn't take a genius to figure out I was being held there against my will.

"Hey, friend." Tom took a step forward, not looking at me at all, but squinting at Clyde. "I just need to talk to Cath for a second. Do you mind?"

"Actually, I do," Clyde replied.

I sighed out loud. This was ridiculous. I was starting to feel very embarrassed as some of the passersby were looking in our direction.

"Okay, no need to make a scene." I balked. "Tom, you've got thirty seconds." I pulled away from Clyde, his fingers still holding on to my jacket as I walked toward the alley on our right. A few steps in, I turned around to look at Tom and hopefully say one thing in words while indicating my real meaning that he needed to leave with my eyes.

"Cath, what in the world is this all about?" he asked, frustration dripping from his words.

"Look. I don't have the time to explain to you." I blinked. I stretched my eyebrows. "Can we just talk tomorrow?"

"Are you in trouble?"

"Of course not." I nodded yes. "Besides, even if I was, I could handle myself. You, of all people, should know that."

"That's enough," Clyde hissed as he blocked the exit from the alley. "I've had enough of this."

"Back off, pal. I'm talking to Cath," Tom said.

"She obviously doesn't want to talk to you. Even if she did, I wouldn't let her."

"You wouldn't let her?" Tom choked out.

"Cath, come with me. We've got to finish our conversation in private." Clyde stepped toward Tom.

"Tom, please. Maybe you could..."

Before I finished my sentence, Clyde swung his arm and made contact with Tom's shoulder, knocking him several feet to my left, where he hit the brick wall with a sickening smack and crumpled in a heap on the dirty ground of the alley.

"What the heck?" I cried and went to check on Tom but was stopped, not making a single successful step, as bony talons clamped around my throat.

Instantly, I tried to swallow, but my muscles wouldn't respond. I tried to breathe, but it was as though I were sucking through a straw. My hands went to the clamps around my throat, and I pulled at them, scratching and yanking, but nothing was pulling these fingers from my throat. He was going to crush my windpipe.

I kicked my legs and looked into Clyde's face, which morphed right in front of me. His teeth elongated. His eyes slipped into blackness like the sun going down on the horizon with a yellow moon iris to stare back at me. His skin turned a sickly yellowish-pink color, and his eyes sank back, creating a fleshy cave that the yellow pinpoints peered out from.

The smell of the alley filled my nose. I couldn't say why my senses became so intense except that I was dying. But I could smell the sickly-sweet tang of the garbage cans. I could feel the moisture bouncing off the ground as just enough precipitation fell between the buildings to dampen everything in the dumpsters and cans and the garbage scattered all over the ground.

"This isn't exactly how I wanted this to go." The Clyde-beast scowled. "But your relatives, Bea and Astrid, will come looking for you soon enough. When you don't make it back to the café tonight, when they don't see you tomorrow or the next day, they'll try their magic to find you. When they do, I'll be waiting."

I continued to scratch at Clyde-beast's hand, struggling to get my fingers beneath his to gasp for some air, but they seemed to get tighter and tighter. Just before I was about to lose consciousness, I heard his voice again.

"Funny how you had Mr. Wayne living here all these years, eating children every December Solstice, and you never suspected a thing. Perhaps his methods were correct all along." The Clyde-beast growled, still looking very much like Clyde Tumble but at the same time resembling the beast in Aunt Astrid's book.

At this new revelation, my eyes snapped open, and I fought away unconsciousness. Did Clyde-beast just say Mr. Wayne and eating children in the same sentence?

Tainted Bloodline

"What does it matter now?" Clyde purred. "I always preferred the chaos, the fear that accompanied my child abductions, especially at this time of the year."

My gosh. How many times had I used that phrase when talking about feeling warm fuzzies and peace on earth and good will to all? Here, Clyde-beast had twisted it into something dirty. I doubt I'd ever be able to utter those words again. I scratched at his hand around my throat.

"How?" I choked the word out, but it sounded as if I were saying "ow." That applied too. Being choked hurt.

"What did you say?" He slightly loosened his grip and yanked my head toward his ear.

He was still on two legs like a man. It was obvious he didn't plan to fully transform into his real shape. He let me just see a shadow of what he really was, like looking into the sky and seeing the crescent moon.

"How—" I gasped, taking in a huge gulp of air. I tried to kick my legs, but they felt as if someone had attached lead weights to them.

"How?" He grinned, exposing more teeth that lined his mouth like those of a shark. He raised his other hand and pointed to the sky. "Mr. Gale Wayne fed off runaways and transient children from Portland and Salem and Medford. Wherever there were troubled teens, he could be found." Clyde-beast chortled. It sounded like a phlegmy, bubbling soup in his throat.

My mind kept drifting toward blackness but was painfully shocked into brutal awareness every couple of seconds. I was sure I was never going to get out of this alive. I stretched my eyes to see if Tom was all right, but he was still lying there on the filthy ground.

"You see." Clyde-beast stepped farther and farther into the alley, the shadows slowly consuming both of us as he whispered the horrifying tale of his kindred spirit, Mr. Wayne, and why he had to be

destroyed. "Mr. Wayne wasn't the innocent perse-
cuted teacher from Bibich High School that you
might have thought. In fact, it was his journeys to
far-off cities that ended up being his undoing. Those
kids who live underneath bridges and sleep in the
bus station are sharp as tacks. Well, some of them
are. And they watch out for each other. It only makes
sense, right? They are on the street, after all. No
warm beds. No television or food whenever they
want it. These kids know the value of looking behind
every once in a while as you walk the streets
at night."

He released my throat, and I slammed to the
ground, feeling my elbow shatter against the
concrete and cobblestone. The flash was white,
searing pain that snapped me awake, forcing tears
into my eyes as I gurgled pitifully.

"One of those children had a friend visiting. That
boy Bruce Lyle had a cousin who was a troubled boy.
Bruce often paid his cousin a simple visit, slumming
it with him as they smoked pot and stayed out all
night. Mr. Wayne pulled up in that piece of garbage
car of his and asked the boys if they needed a ride
before realizing one of them was a student.
Nice, right?"

"He was going to murder them." I didn't recognize my own voice. As if I'd smoked over twenty packs of cigarettes within the last half hour, my voice was gravelly, and the words painfully scraped my throat as they came out.

"That he was." The Clyde-beast towered over me. I wanted to run. My gut was telling me to just push off and bolt in any direction. "But he lost his composure when little Bruce Lyle recognized him and said his name out loud. That kid thought Mr. Wayne was one of those kiddie molesters. Little did he know he was so wrong."

Clyde's hands furled and unfurled as he began panting, his broad shoulders hulking up and down and his face looming down at me. Those eyes, like sick cat eyes, looked deep into mine. My lower lip trembled.

"But it was too late now. That was how the rumors at the school started." Clyde-beast smiled.

"When I heard from my brethren, the few of us that are left, what was happening, I thought it was time for me to relocate. Why not, right? Do you know how easy it is to become a substitute teacher? Obtaining a certificate that says you are qualified to mold young minds is easier than getting a library card." He laughed that thick, foamy laugh again. "As a substitute teacher, I had access to all of them. Each and every child in the area followed me like the Pied Piper. It was almost shameful the way they'd vie for my attention. I could devour seven, eight, maybe even nine of them before the Winter Solstice was over, and I'd be satiated until the following year. The case would run cold. The police would forget details, be transferred, retire, quit. Each year when my killings started, it would be like a whole new ball of wax for the local police. They'd never catch me. They hadn't so far."

"How did you get Mr. Wayne to commit suicide? He obviously was not quite like you," I spat.

"He didn't commit suicide." The Clyde-beast disappeared in front of my eyes then reappeared almost instantly. "It was so easy to make it look that way. I killed the Lyle boy and some girl and left their bodies where the police would naturally put two and two together. Suicide was the only way to get them to stop investigating. And they did."

"But you didn't expect us," I hissed. Blinking, I tried to focus and saw a simmering hatred immediately turn into a rolling boil.

"When I discovered Mr. Wayne had been living in the same town as Greenstones, as the tainted bloodline that thought it had gotten rid of my kind, well, let's just say I was perturbed."

The Clyde-beast reached down and grabbed a handful of my hair. Before he yanked me to my feet, I picked out a tiny shard of green glass from a broken bottle and cupped it in my limp hand as my good arm slapped on top of his bony fingers in an attempt to relax the pain. It didn't work.

"He knew who you were but did nothing. He even ate your food. Visited your business. He could have slaughtered you all in mere seconds and escaped easily. But he obviously enjoyed his human skin more than his true form. Disgusting!" The Clyde-beast spat the words in my ear, and I could feel his hot breath on my cheek and detected the smell of rotting meat there, too.

"So not all of you creatures are evil. Just the ones that smell like you? That hot-garbage smell? Is that it? Well, I know I might not make it, but I can tell you one thing for sure." I dug my nails into his claw and leaned forward as best I could, looking the creature in its feverish eyes. "Neither will you."

With pain so intense I was afraid I might pass out, I lifted my busted-up arm and pierced the fleshy part of the Clyde-beast's hand. He threw his head back in pain, howling like... well, like a wounded cat, releasing my hair and once again dropping me to the ground.

Except this time I didn't land on my elbow. I landed on my feet, albeit awkwardly, and tumbled backward, landing on a pile of garbage bags. Thankfully, they were tied shut, as whatever was inside them felt gushy, as if it was in between turning from a solid to a liquid.

The Clyde-beast grasped its injured hand and scowled at me as it proceeded to continue its grotesque transformation. It was no longer the Clyde-beast. It was now The Beast.

Lair

❧❦☙

Aunt Astrid's description of the giant hairless cat failed to really capture not just the immensity of the monster, but also the diabolical aura around it. I held my breath as it waved its hands, muttering some words human ears were never meant to hear.

The air around me became heavy. I was still breathing, but I felt as if I were underwater. The snowflakes that had been falling stopped in midair. The sounds of the busy street just outside the open mouth of the alley had ceased.

I was alone, and my heartbeat was the only sound I could hear. My mouth was totally dry, and I was hot and cold beneath my coat.

"You'll pay for that!" it cried out. "But don't worry.

I'm not going to kill you. Not yet. I'll give you a chance to say good-bye to your family. You'll watch me tear them apart piece by piece. Only after you've heard them beg for their lives, after you've seen madness from the agony consume them, will you finally be released from this plane of existence. And I will go on."

The Beast lunged at me, but before its long arms could get ahold of me, my hero jumped in front of him, ready for battle.

"You talk too much," Treacle said, his fur on end, his eyes narrow and sparkling and his claws extended.

"You again. I knew I'd see you, but I was sure it would be long after your master was trampled under my feet." The Beast spoke with Treacle, unaware that I could hear it.

Treacle was not even a third the size of the Beast, yet he looked his equal. His black coat glistened with a healthy, strong glow compared to the sickly hue of the skin on the monster. My cat was fully alive with an excited, beating heart and a sharp mind that wouldn't be taken in by this devil.

"You don't really think you can stop me," the Beast hissed as it slowly began to arch its back. *"But I'll tell you what. I'll let her live if you join me."*

"Join you?" Treacle crossed his right front paw over his left as he slowly circled to the right.

"Imagine it," the Beast meowed. *"Having the power to come and go as you please not only in this world, but in a thousand more. You'll be feared and worshipped. Sacrifices will be made to you, and when they aren't, you'll be able to feed on the nonbelievers. Like here in this place."*

Treacle took a step back.

"Yes. Think about it," the Beast continued. *"I'll let her live if you join me. Together, we'll sacrifice the other Greenstones, and this one can live knowing it was due to you she was spared."*

Treacle looked back at me.

"You really do talk too much. Marshmallow! PB! We're down here!"

"Where are they?" I asked telepathically.

"Oh, they're not far and they're ready to fight."

"What? You tricked me!" The hairless cat snarled furiously.

"I heard you all this time. What did you think? I was a Greenstone without any powers?" I got to my feet.

There was movement out of the corner of my eye. It was the rest of the cavalry.

Marshmallow and Peanut Butter bolted down the alley and stopped behind Treacle. I had never seen

Peanut Butter so furious as he was just then. Hissing and clawing at the ground, he was ready for battle.

Then I gasped as Aunt Astrid and Bea brought up the rear. My aunt was holding open a book that looked as if the pages had been sprinkled with rusty water. The words were Celtic in nature—at least I thought they were.

As she came to my side, the hairless beast hissed and swiped at all of us. Its eyes glowed with anger and revenge. Waving its arms again, choking out more horrible-sounding words, it arched its back as if it was getting ready to pounce on all of us.

I looked at my aunt, whose eyes had grown wide.

"What is it?" I cried.

"He's opened another portal. The one to his lair," she muttered, her eyes focusing with determination. "Let's shut that once and for all."

The Beast took a swipe in our direction, just missing me.

Treacle cried out, and all three cats jumped at the Beast, clinging to its naked skin with their thin, needlelike claws and sinking their teeth into the flesh. The Beast cried out in agony. Bea slipped by, stepping on the garbage bags that had broken my fall, and linked her arm with mine as she stood up straight and watched as our cats fought for the precious moments needed for my aunt to read.

"How did you know to come?" I asked, never taking my eyes off the hissing monster as it whipped its tail and clawed at the cats. They managed to stay in spots it couldn't reach. But I saw Treacle inching his way toward the thing's neck.

"Treacle! Be careful!" I screamed without saying a word out loud.

As if on cue, the hairless cat reached up and tried to grab him by the head.

I screamed.

"Dul amach! Dul ar shiul! Powers of the universe make it so! *Dul amach! Dul ar shiul!"* My aunt stood straight and still as she stared down the monster, which twisted and contorted as our pets continued to cling to its skin. By now, trails of blood were dripping down its skin, turning its sickly-pink color a disturbing blotchy red mess.

We all stood there and waited.

"What's supposed to happen?" I asked.

"He's supposed to shrivel up and die," Bea replied.

"I'm not seeing any additional wrinkles to indicate he's shriveling," I whined. "Aunt Astrid, I don't think he's shriveling." My voice trembled.

Quickly, my aunt looked down at her book.

"I don't know what's wrong." Her fingers slid down the passage. Her eyes scanned the words as she looked for something, but she didn't know what. "This should have worked."

The hairless cat began to laugh. Through the torturous bites and scratching from our familiars, it laughed and stood up on its hind legs, shaking its body until Peanut Butter and Marshmallow went flying in opposite directions. Treacle held fast.

I stared in terror as the beast grinned at me.

"I won't kill him," he taunted me. *"I'll just make him my slave."*

"No!" I screamed out loud as the Beast easily pulled Treacle off his neck with his viselike claws and held him dangling helplessly in the air.

I saw the kitten I had adopted all those years ago. My eyes filled with tears, and I barely heard myself as I begged he not hurt my cat. I offered my soul, my body, everything as Bea held me back from approaching too close to this creature that couldn't be trusted. "Don't hurt him! Please don't hurt him!"

"Don't worry. He'll learn to serve with three legs," it mocked me then laughed at me as I screamed.

I was snapped out of my terror by the sound of a gunshot.

Clyde Tumble, aka The Beast, let out a horrific shriek of pain and anger as he dropped Treacle and clutched at the wound in his heart.

Aunt Astrid, Bea, and I turned in the direction of the flash and bang and saw Tom leaning against the brick wall of the building behind us, his face streaked with blood and his left arm bent against his stomach. His right arm remained stiff and straight in front of him, holding the gun.

Quickly, my aunt looked down at her pages and yelped a eureka.

"*Dul amach! Dul ar shiul! Dul amach! Dul ar shiul!* Powers of the universe make it so! *Dul amach! Dul ar shiul!*"

At that moment, the monster began to transform again. It melted and contorted from the giant hairless cat to Clyde Tumble to a shimmering, clear blob, then back again.

The molting became so quick that it began to blend the bodies together into a grotesque abomination until finally it froze in one agonizing grimace with only its eyes moving. They seethed with hatred as Bea approached, her hands extended while she mouthed an ancient invocation that would release the creature's soul from its sick and twisted body.

Treacle had landed on his feet, but he was shaking and sneezing. I scooped him up.

Bea continued her chant as Aunt Astrid repeated her mantra as well.

I noticed movement down the alley, and as I focused, I saw the glinting green and yellow and red eyes of over a dozen stray cats carefully padding their way toward the spectacle that was taking place.

"I thought we might need backup," Treacle purred then jumped from my arms.

"We sure could," I replied. Then I raised my hands and recited my own incantation to bind the monster to one form.

"The cat went here and there, and the moon twirled round like a top, and the nearest kinfolk of the moon, the slinking cat, looked up."

The skin of what had been Clyde Tumble turned rough as if it were drying out. What had before been a terrifyingly gross hairless cat began to shrivel and dry up like a worm left struggling on hot pavement after rain.

Treacle and his friends, including Marshmallow and Peanut Butter, encircled the creature, and as it tried to flee, it was bitterly cut off by their fierce hisses and extended claws. It continued to fold in on itself, but none of us thought for a moment that it wasn't going to try one more stunt.

Bea ran to her mother, and from somewhere inside the folds of my aunt's billowing coat, she pulled out a bag of salt. Quickly, she sprinkled it just in front of all the cats, making sure they did not get trapped in the sacred circle with it. It would have meant a painful and long death if any of them were to get trapped with the Beast.

The only problem was that as each cat stepped aside for the salt to be poured, the giant cat tried to slink through the opening, which was becoming narrower by the second.

"Careful, Bea!" I shouted as one of those giant claws took a swipe, catching Bea's coat with the tiniest razor point of its claw.

Guardians

❧

Thinking as quickly as I could under these circumstances, I looked behind me and spring-heeled over the garbage bags to get a two-by-four. Before fear or common sense could enter into my mind, I swung the wood as if I were taking a golf swing and not only released Bea from its slimy, deadly grasp, but also felt the bony fingers crack like dried acorns.

The monster howled in agony. Its black-and-yellow eyes narrowed at me, but as it leaned back on its haunches as if it was getting ready to pounce on me, it folded even further in on itself. It hissed, swiping at us all as though we were tiny gnats swarming around its head.

Finally, Bea completed the circle, the cats took

their places, sitting nobly like guardians, and we all watched as Clyde Tumble-giant-hairless-cat-invisible-demon burst into flames. Its arms and legs and tail curled up onto themselves, and its head rolled and snapped back and forth before it disappeared in a rather small pop of embers.

The snowflakes began to fall like normal again. The sounds of the busy streets and Christmas music could be heard from the ends of the alley. Treacle, Marshmallow, and Peanut Butter nuzzled each other before Treacle made the rounds to each stray and outdoor cat that had made it to the event.

"*I don't know how to thank you all,*" I said to the small army of felines. "*We probably wouldn't have succeeded if you hadn't shown up.*"

"*We know who you are, Greenstone. It's what we're here for,*" one especially large gray-striped shorthair cat replied to me. He had one bad eye, and I could see several bites had been taken from his ears. His feet were dirty. Without saying another word, he and the other cats slinked away in all directions, blending into the shadows to continue their evening prowl. I looked down at Treacle, who leaned against my leg.

"*My gosh.*" I held back tears. "*I'll carry you home.*"

"*I think you have someone else who needs your help more.*" Treacle pushed his head hard against my leg then trotted over to Tom, who was leaning against the brick wall, the gun still in his hand, still not believing what his eyes had just seen.

"Bea." I clutched my cousin's arm. She was staring at the charred ashes that were all that remained in the center of the circle of salt.

"I wondered why that man would never come into the café," Aunt Astrid spat with disgust. "The night he appeared as the cat, I had sprinkled salt all around. It was still there. I left it, just a very thin trail, and it was enough to keep him out. I should have pieced that together sooner."

"Bea, please." I gently pulled her sleeve. "Tom is hurt."

Bea snapped out of her trance and looked at me. I pointed in his direction. Without a word, Bea went over to him.

"Tom, are you all right?" she asked kindly. I stood behind her with Treacle at my feet. Both Marshmallow and Peanut Butter stood on either side of my aunt like brave little guardians.

"I don't know," he replied. He didn't look at me. He sort of stared around randomly. I knew that look. I'd seen it before. My heart cracked on the inside, but I kept my face brave and serious.

"He's going to be okay, isn't he?" Treacle asked me.

"*I think he'll recover from this. Yes. But we probably won't be seeing too much of him anymore.*" I watched as Tom reluctantly let Bea push and pull the air around his head, moving and adjusting things he couldn't see.

"There you are," Bea muttered forcefully. "Time to go." She put her hand firmly on Tom's shoulder and, with a sudden snap, altered his aura in order to let the energy flow and allow proper healing to start. "You should still go to the emergency room. You'll want them to check your head. I don't see any energy blockages, but you might have a concussion."

"You think?"

"I'll go with you, if you want," I offered.

"No." He looked at me sadly. "You should take Treacle home. I'll be fine."

I nodded as if I agreed that was the best idea, but inside, all I could feel were those words bouncing around inside my head, hollow. Did he think I was serious when I was talking to him in front of Clyde Tumble? He had to know I was just saying those things to get him out of there. It was all to keep him safe. He had to know that, right?

"Will you call me and let me know what the doctor tells you?" I was almost pleading.

"He'll let us know," Aunt Astrid interjected sternly.

The look on her face was the same look I often got when I suggested she let me cast a spell on Darla Castellano so that she'd develop a severe case of warts or maybe a pug nose. I wasn't sure what that was about, but it made me think that she had seen something in the near future that she didn't like. I could guess. I was getting dumped. Again.

❧❧

WE ALL WENT BACK TO MY HOUSE, AND I PUT on some coffee, opened a bag of potato chips, pulled out some French onion dip from the fridge, and placed everything on my kitchen table.

"What a night." I sighed, flopping down in my seat, and watched Treacle, Marshmallow, and Peanut Butter make a beeline for my bedroom and cozy up to each other on my bed. Within seconds, they were asleep. "How did you guys know where I was?"

"Right after you left, Tom came to the café. He wanted to see you before he went to work in a couple hours," Bea replied, daintily reaching into the bag of chips. "Well, we didn't want to tell him you'd left with Clyde Tumble. How would that look, right?"

"It would look as bad as it looked." I shrugged.

"Apparently, he saw you both walking at the end of the street." Aunt Astrid folded her arms across her chest. "I told him not to go. I told him that you were handling something, that we were going to be right behind you in just a few minutes and that he should call you tonight. But typical male, he was going to get to the bottom of things on *his* time. It would have been rather charming had it not been so darn dangerous."

"We knew there might be trouble, so we shut down the café and followed Tom, who led us to you, who ultimately brought us to the Diabolus Formarum Catus," Bea added, reaching for her second chip.

"Well, let me tell you what I learned." I relayed the whole elaborate plot that Mr. Tumble had put in motion to not just frame Mr. Wayne, but also to end the Greenstone lineage once and for all.

"Wow." Bea helped herself to a handful of chips and dipped them in the French onion dip one at a time. "So Mr. Wayne was framed for killing Bruce and Donna, whom he *didn't* kill, but who knows how many children he *did* kill over the years. I'm having a hard time feeling bad for him."

"My question is how did you know what spell to read?" I put my hand over my aunt's hand across the table.

"The Diabolus Formarum Catus was thought to be extinct. The Greenstones were the ones who last encountered them, and each Catus met a similar demise as our friend Mr. Tumble. However, as they are masters of hiddenness, invisibility, I'm not surprised that a few may have been missed."

"But that still doesn't explain how you knew what spell to use."

"We had been searching the textbooks and found what the creature was." She smiled at me. "It was only when I thought that a member of my family, someone as close to me as my own daughter, was in grave danger, that I thought there might be an answer in our family records. I was right."

"How come it didn't work the first time you read it?" Bea asked with a mouth full of chips.

"Oh, um. Well, I was supposed to read it twice, and in my haste, I neglected to do so." Aunt Astrid pushed her hair aside and let out a deep breath.

"You read it wrong?" I smirked. "We were about

to become human Fancy Feast, and you read the spell wrong?"

"That's very amateurish, Mom. I hate to say it."

"But it didn't *stop* you from saying it." Aunt Astrid pointed at her daughter, her blue eyes twinkling.

We sat there quietly for a moment, and suddenly I felt all eyes on me.

"What?"

"You seem a little sad, Cath." Bea put her hand on mine. "Are you okay?"

"Yeah." I blinked, my eyes getting a little teary. "I finally figured out what to get Tom for Christmas, and now it looks like he's going the way of the dodo bird. I'm just a little bummed. That's all."

"You don't know that for sure." Bea took another chip. "He knows what being involved with a Greenstone entails. He didn't seem at all intimidated by it."

"Yeah, but I said some things to him."

"What things?" My aunt looked at me understandingly.

"Mr. Tumble was there. I knew things were going to go sideways, and Tom just wouldn't listen. He kept acting all jealous and worried and angry, and so I basically told him to take a hike." I shook my head while staring at my hands in my lap. "I didn't mean it. He just wouldn't listen. I didn't want him to get hurt, and what happened? He ended up getting hurt anyways and now is probably at the hospital, flirting with an average, run-of-the-mill emergency room nurse who doesn't believe in ghosts or witches or UFOs or any of that."

I waited for Aunt Astrid and Bea to offer some kind of encouragement. Usually they'd say something like "You're crazy" or "He probably knows you didn't mean it" or "It's his loss." But they didn't say anything, and that made me think that things with Tom were probably done.

"What were you going to give him for Christmas?" Bea nudged me.

"It doesn't matter now."

"Well, sure, it does," my aunt piped up. "There is a reason for the season, and it has nothing to do with Diabolus Formarum Catus. It has to do with miracles and mysteries and those things we may not understand but believe in."

I looked at my aunt as she smiled at me.

"It can be a solitary, thankless job being a witch. But there are those men out there who were picked by the Great Creator to stand by us. If Tom is one of those exceptional men, I don't know. But head into it like he is, Cath. If he proves he isn't your knight in shining armor, be assured that one is out there just waiting to slay a dragon for you."

I hugged my aunt. Then I took the bag of chips away from Bea before she overdosed on GMOs.

Comfy and Crinkly

❦

"**A**ren't you going to answer that?" Treacle nudged my cellphone toward me on the floor as I struggled with an unruly roll of wrapping paper.

"Nope."

"Well, at least tell me who it is that you are avoiding."

"It's Tom." I sighed. "He's just calling to tell me that we won't be going to the Policeman's Christmas Ball and that we should probably see other people, or this thing just isn't working out, or whatever. I figured I'd make it easy on him and let him break up with me on voicemail."

"What if he's calling to tell you that he'll be picking you up at six? You won't be ready."

I was not surprised to hear Treacle pleading Tom's case. He loved Tom. There was something the two bonded over. Maybe it was the machismo. Maybe it was the fact they both crept around alleys. I don't know. But I could tell Treacle was a little nervous his buddy might not be coming around as much anymore.

"Fine. You want me to prove it to you?" I picked up the phone, dialed my voicemail, and hit speaker. "Here you go."

"Hi, Cath. It's Tom. Look, I'm sorry to do this last minute, but I don't think we can go to the Christmas Ball. I was..."

Not wanting to hear any more, I hit the delete button and then shut off the phone. Treacle came and sat right in front of me on the very wrapping paper I was trying to manipulate around a long, rectangular box.

"*I'm sorry,*" he purred.

"It's not your fault. In fact, truthfully, Tom should come and say a special thank-you to you and all your rowdy friends for taking on the Big Nasty like you did." I scratched behind his ears.

"*Are you going to talk to him again?*"

"Well, I'm going to take Aunt Astrid's advice. I'm going to wrap up his Christmas present, and if I don't see him in the next couple of days, I'll just mail it off to him. Maybe he'll like it. Maybe he'll hate it.

But at least I can tell him that I wish him all the best. Right? I don't have to be a Scrooge about it all." I sat back and frowned.

"*What is it?*"

"I swear if I see him walking with Darla Castellano hanging on his arm, I'm going to lose my mind. That would just be too much. I still can't get over the fact that Blake went out with her. Talk about going from the frying pan into the fire."

I looked down at my cat and pushed my forehead into his.

"Can I have this now?" I asked, tugging at the wrapping paper.

"*Now? You want it now?*"

"I need to finish up. Come on."

"*No. I don't think so. It's so comfy and crinkly.*"

"*Treacle, you're a big kitty now. You don't do things like play with rolls of wrapping paper.*" I pulled a new roll of paper from the plastic wrapping it was in and tossed it across the floor.

The temptation was just too great. Within seconds, Treacle was facing the unsuspecting roll, butt wiggling, eyes staring. He dashed into the paper, his black arms extended in front of him, his haunches staying close to the ground as he pushed the paper until it completely unfurled and the long cardboard tube was left naked.

"You want some bows to go with that?" I asked, getting back to my own project.

"I'm good with this!" he shouted as he darted, pounced, scratched, and crumpled the unused wrapping paper until, satisfied he had established his authority over it, he curled up in a contented black ball of fur right in the middle of the crinkling mess. I laughed. I couldn't help myself.

Pictures

T he night of the Policeman's Ball came and went. To shake my blues, I had gone to a thrift store and actually found a lovely green dress. It was a little over the top in that it had a faux fur collar and cuffs, but when I looked in the mirror after trying it on, I really thought I looked pretty. It isn't often I think I look pretty. Not to harbor any false modesty, it's just that I'm not like Darla Castellano, who wears tons of makeup and has her nails done and all that jazz. I worked. I sometimes fought demons and specters from other dimensions. Primping wasn't a usual part of my daily routine. But for this dress, I was going to pull out all the stops.

The Brew-Ha-Ha had a Christmas party every year, and this time I wasn't going to wear my ugliest

Christmas sweater. Trust me, it was so hideous it should have been a Halloween sweater. It was this headache-inducing purple color with little pearl beads attached all over so leaning on the back of a chair hurt. Taking up the entire front was an embroidered Christmas tree with tacky seed beads and sequins filling in all the branches. The collar was an oversized turtleneck that gave a hint of that *Flashdance*-era off-the-shoulder look, and the hem was black with the same seed beads and sequins sewn around it.

Nope. Not this year. I'd be dressing up this year, and maybe I wouldn't even avoid the mistletoe.

The café was closed during the day before Christmas Eve. The sign on the door read "Closed until 5:00 p.m. Please come back for free coffee and a gingerbread cookie with every food donation to the Wonderfalls Food Pantry. Merry Christmas."

The lights of the café shined warmly out onto the sidewalk. There were lots of people who I knew already there, and I listened for just a few seconds to the laughter and the Christmas music playing in the background.

"Are we going in or will we be admiring the party from out here?" Treacle moaned.

"Can I just savor the moment?" I looked over my

armful of packages at my cat as he stood on the side-walk next to me.

"Are you savoring the moment, or are you stalling?"

"I'm not stalling." I smirked and clicked my tongue. *"Come on, Fuzzy. I'm sure there is a bowl of milk in there with your name on it."*

I pulled the door open, setting off the jingling bells, and was hit with the soothing smell of ginger-bread in addition to a wonderful potpourri of orange, allspice, and vanilla that I knew Bea had put together that was simmering over a small candle on Aunt Astrid's tarot-reading table. The Christmas music was cheery and familiar, bringing back beautiful memories of getting off school for the Christmas break, snow days, and the long wait for Santa to finally come.

"Cath!" Bea squealed as she spun around from the huge stacks of boxes and paper bags filled with food donations. "Look at all the donations so far!"

"My gosh." I set my packages down. "That's wonderful." I pulled off my coat, and I swear the entire place felt as if it were holding its breath.

"Oh my gosh." Bea spun me around. "You look stunning."

That was quite a compliment from my redheaded cousin, who had her hair piled on her head and wore a red tea-length pencil skirt plus a downy white sweater and a big poinsettia pin on her collar.

"Right back at you, sister." I hugged her tightly. "You and Jake, stay away from that mistletoe. This is a family establishment."

"I gave him an early present. He's wearing his candy-cane boxers." Bea giggled hysterically.

"Yay. Too much information. Just what I wanted for Christmas!"

Jake sported a green sweater and a Santa hat. He handed me a glass of eggnog, giving me a peck on the cheek then patting me on the back as if I were one of the guys.

"You look great, Cath." He smiled.

"You, too, Jake. I saw your underwear."

"What?"

"Bea showed them to me after she bought them. Yup. I've seen your festive, yuletide, Christmas undies. Ho ho ho." I laughed as Jake's face turned red.

"You're a riot, cuz." He pinched my arm before slipping over to Bea and shaking his head as she laughed, wrapping her arms around his stomach.

I was able to get a quick hug from Kevin Baker, who was cranking out the gingerbread men in the kitchen with a glass of eggnog at his side, as well as an elaborate goblet that I was pretty sure held my aunt Astrid's recipe for a hot toddy.

Aunt Astrid was pointing to a bunch of old ornaments on the five-foot-tall tree with her arm linked through Blake Samberg's.

"That one Cath made when she was in fifth—no, wait, sixth grade. That one she made in seventh grade. I had one from eighth grade, too, but Peanut Butter got very drunk at one of these Christmas parties and batted it off the branches."

"Merry Christmas." I tapped my aunt on the shoulder.

"Cath, my heavens. What a beautiful dress."

"It's nice, right?" I looked up at Blake, who stood there without saying a word. Typical. I rolled my eyes. "I found it at a thrift store."

"You look so lovely. Wait, I need to find my camera. I know it's around here somewhere." My aunt patted the folds of her maroon-colored gypsy-style dress, pulled the top open, and looked down the top of her dress.

"Is it in there?" I asked, smiling. I was sure my aunt had had a couple sips of her own hot toddy concoction.

"Nope." She smiled and nudged me under the chin. "I think I left it on the counter. You two wait here. I want a picture!" She yelped with excitement.

Blake was wearing the same suit he always wore, but I was surprised to see the red, white, and green striped necktie, and it made me grin.

"Wow, Blake. Getting a little daring with the wardrobe." I flipped his tie with my finger then smoothed it back in place.

"Funny," he muttered. "That's what Jake said."

"Really? Well, I mean it. A little splash of color looks nice on you." I smiled up at him. In return, I got the usual stoic gaze with the left side of his mouth curving up slightly. This was the equivalent of doubled over laughing for Blake Samberg.

"Your aunt was just showing me some of the ornaments you made for her as a kid."

"Oh yeah. I was an aspiring Picasso. Nothing ever looked like it was supposed to, so I would insist that the odd shapes and sizes were my artistic interpretations." I folded my arms and rocked on my heels. "No one bought it. They knew I just wasn't that artistic."

"Kids' artwork is one hundred percent love. That's what makes it beautiful," he said, gently touching a lopsided ceramic Christmas tree I had made. "Homemade gifts really are the best, when you think of it."

"You think so?" I was fascinated.

"Well, think about it. You take the time to think up the gift. You take the time to get your supplies. You take the time to put it all together. And if you're someone like me, usually there is a lot of starting over because you've made mistakes."

I chuckled.

"That's quite a bit of effort that you just don't give to someone who doesn't mean a lot to you." He looked at the ornaments again. "Not to mention you don't have to worry about getting duplicates. I can't tell you how many times I received a red tie for Christmas only to receive a slightly brighter red tie the very next year."

"Maybe you should tell people that you don't need any ties for Christmas," I joked. "Although whoever picked that one out for you went a little wild. Red and green."

"It was your aunt."

"No way!" I shrieked with laughter. "Oh my gosh. I feel so bad for you. Okay, no I don't. I think it is exactly what you deserve."

It was like a Christmas miracle. Blake Samberg actually laughed out loud. It was contagious. I pointed at him and laughed even harder, which seemed to make him do the same.

"My goodness, Blake. People are going to think we're drunk." I sipped my eggnog.

"There are worse things." He looked down at me with those serious eyes, still smiling broadly and taking a sip of his own mug of eggnog.

"Well, I better help my cousin. She's getting a little swamped at the register. Can I hand you some of these grocery bags? It looks like people are really feeling the Christmas spirit this year."

"I'm happy to help."

As the evening went by, with each group of last-minute shoppers who brought in food or gave a couple of bucks, the café rolled along, a happy and safe place for everyone. I don't like to sound like a hippie, but I really could feel the love.

Jake turned up "Jingle Bell Rock" and he and Bea did some swing dancing. I thought I was going to split a gut as Blake, with his serious and stonelike face, stood next to Aunt Astrid, doing the twist while she rocked back and forth, oblivious to his shenanigans.

More customers with familiar faces came in to chitchat and enjoy the festivities, and I got more compliments on my dress than ever before in my life.

Min Park made a long-distance call from Hawaii to talk to me and tell me to watch the mail. A coconut postcard would be arriving within the next few days. That sounded like code for some weird, secret government package, but as it turned out, I really did receive a huge brown, bulky coconut post-card from Hawaii. It was awesome.

But I will admit that every time the door jingled, I looked up and hoped it was Tom. Even through all the laughter and singing and visits with friends from the neighborhood, I was a little lonely. When I got this way, I looked for Treacle. He, Peanut Butter, and Marshmallow had each perched themselves on a bookshelf, looking down at all the revelers like feline gods and goddesses. I walked over and gave each one a scratch under the chin, wishing them Merry Christ-mas, to which they purred their reply.

"Okay. It's picture time," my aunt announced. "Now, everyone crowd together, and I'll get all you lunatics at once."

We laughed as we huddled together, Bea and I in the center, holding hands like sisters and looking as complementary as ever in our red and green. My aunt, trying to sort through this dimension and the others she could see, laughed and instructed Jake to stand up straight and me to move a little to the side and Blake to stoop down a little and Kevin to come forward and Bea to scoot back until finally it was perfect and she snapped away.

She had Jake take one of the three Greenstone women. Of course, Bea and Jake posed as though they were at prom and the teachers weren't looking, getting all lovey-dovey and gazing with dreamy eyes at each other. Then Jake and Blake stood together, thankful they were partners on the force and thankful they were alive after some of the experiences they had over the year. Kevin posed with the never-ending goblet of toddy at the oven in the kitchen, and even the cats stayed on their shelves for a couple of quick shots before hopping down to investigate the fresh green catnip plants Jake had for each of them.

"So it looks like it's just you and me, cowboy," I muttered to Blake as my aunt adjusted her camera.

"Why don't you let her take a picture of you alone first. I'm sure she'd like to remember you in that dress."

Yes, my cheeks flushed. Of course they flushed. Anyone's cheeks would blaze up at a comment like that. I posed for my aunt, who was eyeing me suspiciously with her own smirk on her lips.

"You two stand over there by the entrance to the basement. And jazz it up. This ain't no funeral."

"Oh my gosh. My aunt is drunk," I muttered.

"Then we better do as she says." Blake took my hand and led me over to the basement door. But before I could strike a stiff and awkward pose with Detective Blake Samberg, the man I love to hate, I saw him point up.

I looked at what he was showing me and swallowed hard. Mistletoe.

Merry Christmas

B efore a snide remark or sarcastic quip could enter into my brain, Blake Samberg slipped his arm around my waist, dipped me backward, and kissed me full on the lips. I heard my aunt's fancy camera snap the picture, forever documenting the moment as well as Bea and Jake and several customers whooping and clapping and carrying on as though they'd never seen a romantic, sweeping kiss ever in their lives.

When he lifted me back up, I wanted to die. No, I didn't. I wanted to do it again, but I'd never breathe a word of that to any soul, living or dead. Not even Treacle would know that the urge to continue that kiss ever existed.

"Merry Christmas, Cath," he whispered, his own

cheeks slightly pinker than normal, and there was a silly grin on his lips.

"Merry Christmas, Blake."

Coolly, he adjusted his tie and swaggered back toward Aunt Astrid, whom he whispered something to, and then went and grabbed his coat. I went to my aunt to review all the photos she had taken over the course of the night, keeping Blake in the corner of my eye.

"Please reconsider coming by for Christmas dinner," Aunt Astrid said as Blake came to give her a hug good-bye.

"I'll do my best." He smiled and kissed her on top of her head. He gave me a wink that I found a little suspicious and planned to interrogate my aunt at the soonest opportunity. But for now I only had one question for her as Blake walked out the door, adjusted his collar, and thrust his hands in his pockets as he headed toward his old car.

"What did he whisper to you?" I folded my arms. "And don't try to lie. I can do a binding spell, too."

"He wanted a copy of that photo of the two of you." She said it as though he had asked for a slice of pie to take home.

"Oh."

"Something wrong?" She looked at me, and I was

HARPER LIN

sure she knew what I swore I'd never tell. That was that I wanted that kiss to continue.

"No." I raised my eyebrows and shrugged. "It's just kind of funny since my present for Tom…"

It was almost eleven o'clock at night. Another half an hour, and I would have been home with my Christmas tree lights on, snuggled in my jammies, with Treacle on the bed, *It's A Wonderful Life* playing on the television until I fell asleep. But Tom made it in just in time.

"Merry Christmas," I said carefully.

Tom looked me up and down, and I was sure after all the night's festivities and excitement that I looked a fright. If I did, he liked it.

"Merry Christmas, Cath. You look beautiful."

"Tom, better late than never." Jake clapped him on the back. "Let me help you with those." He took a large grocery bag from Tom's good arm and placed it with the arsenal of others we had collected. But not before knocking on the cast that he had on his other arm.

Aunt Astrid and Bea gave him big holiday hugs, and even Kevin came out of the kitchen for a minute to give Tom a hug and warn him against my aunt's holiday potion.

Finally, everyone left us alone.

"You didn't call me back." He stared at me. "I was afraid you were mad at me for following you and trying to help with that big, uh, thing." He frowned.

"I got your message that we weren't going to the Policeman's Ball. I thought you were calling it quits because of that big, uh, thing."

"I don't understand. I said we weren't going because the medicine the docs gave me was too strong and I didn't want to look drunk or inebriated while I was with you." Tom blinked. "Everyone would think you drugged me in order to take advantage of me."

"What?" I snapped. "You didn't say that." Then I snapped my fingers. "Wait. I didn't listen to the whole message. I thought you were giving me the boot, so when I heard you say we weren't going to the ball, I just assumed that was the end of it."

"Are you crazy, Cath Greenstone? Is that your problem?" Tom pulled off his jacket and winced as it got caught on the cast.

"Wait," I barked again, frustrated with myself and embarrassed over the whole situation. "Let me help you with your jacket. You want some eggnog?"

Tom smiled that devilish, sly smile. He was loving every minute that I was squirming and slowly nodded as he took a seat at the counter. I came back with two glasses that we clinked together and toasted to our stupidity.

"Do you really think I believed you were going to dump me for a guy like Clyde?" Tom teased. "You are going to have to try a little harder than a couple of harsh words to get me to turn tail."

"But Aunt Astrid said that you were mad and looking for me, and when you saw me walking with him, you just went all Rambo-testosterone-alpha-male."

"Well, I might have been a little bit jealous for a split second." He sipped his eggnog and raised his eyebrows. "Had I seen you in this dress first, I would have been insanely jealous."

"I bought this for the ball," I said, smoothing my skirt. "That no one took me to. All dressed up and nowhere to go, I guess."

"You look beautiful."

"Thank you." My eyes popped open, and I hopped off the stool. "I have something for you." I dug into my purse and pulled out the rectangular box I had been struggling to wrap.

"For me?" Tom smiled.

"No. For your Aunt Tilly. Yes, for you."

He furrowed his brow and clicked his tongue at

my sarcasm, making me laugh as I quickly refilled his mug with eggnog.

"It's okay if you don't like it. I didn't want to get you a tie."

Tom stared into the box with the tissue paper pulled aside and said nothing.

"I hope I'm not making you uncomfortable," I said, not sure how to read his reaction. "I mean, buying for girls is so much easier. We all like pretty things and stuff that smells good. You dudes can be pretty tricky." I swallowed hard.

"What have you got there, Tom?" Bea asked innocently as she scooted behind the counter.

"Cath's present." Tom grinned and wiped a tear from his cheek.

Bea looked at me quickly then leaned over the counter.

"What is it? She didn't tell any of us."

Tom pulled the simple gilded frame out of the box and held it up for Bea.

"Cath." She gasped. "That's beautiful."

In the frame was a black-and-white picture of Treacle and me, surrounded by a forest-green matte.

"It's not too snooty, right, to give you a picture of us?"

Tom shook his head.

"Because I asked Bea, and she was so busy buying Christmas socks and drawers for Jake that she really wasn't any help."

"Advertise it, why don't you," Bea sniffed.

"Why not? *You* did," I snapped back, making her laugh as she put on a cup of coffee. "I just thought that even if these things that have been happening between us—I'm talking about the bug-a-boos and heebie-jeebies—even if they get to be too much for you, I hope we'll always be friends."

"I hope we'll always be more than that." Tom leaned over and kissed me. My heart exploded in my chest, and I wanted to cry and laugh and sing off-key, all at the same time. In that moment, I heard the sound of trumpets and choirs singing and even jingling bells. Okay, it was the music over the speakers, but it was nonetheless inspiring.

When I leaned back and caught my breath, I realized the door had opened and closed quickly, causing those bells to jingle.

"Every time a bell rings, an angel gets its wings," I recited the famous line. "Name that movie, Bea." I looked at my cousin, who had a sad look on her face. "You okay? What's the matter?"

"Oh, no." She shook her head and smiled brightly. "I was just thinking of all the folks who don't have enough food and how maybe we helped just a little tonight." She jerked her thumb at the mountain of food collected for the Wonder Falls Food Pantry.

"I can help you deliver it all," Tom volunteered. "All that should fit just right in the back of my truck. When do they need it by?"

"Really, Tom? It's no trouble?" I asked.

"I'll just need someone else to load it, but it won't be any problem at all." He pushed a stray strand of hair from my cheek.

"Well, all right." I hopped off the stool and recruited Jake and Kevin to load everything onto the truck. Bea had called Mrs. Wimby, the woman who oversaw all the donations at WFP. They were indeed open late due to all the last-minute givers who got the Christmas spirit at the eleventh hour.

Once everything was loaded, I kissed everyone good night, even Kevin Baker, and climbed aboard Tom's trusty steed with four wheels and headed off to the food pantry. Maybe the dragon he was ready to slay was a monster of my own making. That creature of pessimism and negativity and isolation tried to rear its head, and in just a few words, Tom lopped off its head.

I felt my own miracle. It was tiny and wouldn't

change the course of the world as the real Christmas miracle off in a tiny manger did. But it didn't make it any less wonderful. I finally felt as if it was possible for me to have a normal life. Well, not normal-normal. No Greenstone could ever have a normal life. It was impossible.

I meant a life like my mother had, like Aunt Astrid had, like Bea had. I could have someone in my life who accepted me as a witch—should I say it? Warts and all? I just did. Not only did he accept it, but he also respected it. If that wasn't a miracle, I don't know what is.

After we dropped off the food at the pantry, we went back to my house and, over hot popcorn and root beer, sat together on my cozy couch, watching *It's a Wonderful Life* while talking about our families and our traditions and our histories and the future.

Outside, the snow started to fall, and soon the entire world was covered in a pristine blanket of white.

෫෯෨

IT WASN'T UNTIL AUNT ASTRID GOT HER pictures developed after the New Year that I saw Blake had been looking at me in each picture I was in. It also wasn't until then that Bea told me he had walked in at the exact moment Tom was kissing me for my Christmas gift.

"He turned and left," she said. "He looked heartbroken."

I took Aunt Astrid's pictures and flipped through them casually while my brain whirred.

"He had his chance, didn't he?" I asked innocently.

About the Author

Harper Lin is the *USA TODAY* bestselling author of 6 cozy mystery series including *The Patisserie Mysteries* and *The Cape Bay Cafe Mysteries*.

When she's not reading or writing mysteries, she loves going to yoga class, hiking, and hanging out with her family and friends.

www.HarperLin.com